T0313549

Silken
Gazelles

JOKHA ALHARTHI

Silken
Gazelles

Translated from the Arabic
by Marilyn Booth

SCRIBNER

LONDON NEW YORK SYDNEY TORONTO NEW DELHI

First published in the United States by Catapult, 2024

Published in Great Britain by Scribner, an imprint of
Simon & Schuster UK Ltd, 2024

SCRIBNER and design are registered trademarks of The Gale Group, Inc.,
used under licence by Simon & Schuster Inc.

1 3 5 7 9 10 8 6 4 2

Simon & Schuster UK Ltd
1st Floor
222 Gray's Inn Road
London WC1X 8HB

Simon & Schuster Australia,
Sydney

Simon & Schuster India,
New Delhi

Simon & Schuster: Celebrating 100 Years of Publishing in 2024

www.simonandschuster.co.uk
www.simonandschuster.com.au
www.simonandschuster.co.in

A CIP catalogue record for this book is available from the British Library

Hardback ISBN: 978-1-3985-2829-1
eBook ISBN: 978-1-3985-2830-7
eAudio ISBN: 978-1-3985-4142-9

Printed and Bound in the UK using 100% Renewable Electricity at
CPI Group (UK) Ltd

MIX
Paper | Supporting
responsible forestry
FSC® C171272

To Mohamed Al Harthi

in his absence, he is always here

Contents

Concert

The green jeep was approaching the village of Sharaat Bat, when a swirling cloud of dust ahead of it announced a cluster of women in mourning hurrying toward the vehicle. The jeep came to a sudden stop and the women encircled it. Pushing back the long tarhas draping their heads, they began to wail. "Woe, aah Fathiya, the blackness of your night! Aah, poor dear—for what you have lost."

As Fathiya scrambled out of the jeep, the nursing infant's mouth slipped off her nipple. "Who?!" she screamed. The women responded in unison. "Your father, orphan girl! We mourn for you, poor sad Fathiya!" The young woman's arms jerked upward and pitched into the air the cloth bundle she had been clasping. She pressed her open palms to her head and gave a loud wail. The baby girl flew out of the swaddling clothes and landed in the arms of one of the mourners. A

3

thin stream of milk welled from Fathiya's uncovered breast and muddied the dirt at her feet.

Days later, Fathiya began to come out of the haze of bewildered grief that had knocked her comatose. She had no idea how much time had passed—day had blended into night. Emerging into consciousness, she remembered the little bundle and the milk that had hardened into lumps before her breasts had gone dry. The women who were gathered around her mat to console her heard her whisper, "The girl. Where's the girl?" These neighbors reassured her. Saada had taken the newborn into her care. Fathiya asked for her, and the baby was returned to its mother.

Saada had snatched the baby as it bobbed momentarily in midair, seemingly caught on a branch—but this must have been a branch on a tree that the wind itself had created. She hung there in the air, her wrappings half undone and falling off, an infant deprived of her milk and cast out of the circle of mourning. And then Saada opened her arms and reached high and picked the baby off her perch. Mouth wide open, the baby was screaming, though her screams were submerged in the women's loudly repeated proclamations that her mother was now fatherless. Saada gave the baby her breast and so the newborn became a milk-sister to ten-month-old Asiya.

Ghazaala. Gazelle. That was the name Saada gave her as she took the baby into her embrace and commenced nursing her. When her own mother returned to her senses and had the baby brought to her, Fathiya named her Layla. On the birth certificate she was recorded as Layla, and that was how her name would appear on her school reports and diplomas over the years. Apart from the birth certificate and her school documents, though, as a child practically no one but her mother called her Layla.

She always believed that her own mother must really be named Saada. And the woman whom everyone called Saada must actually be Fathiya. She did not know how to explain any of this mix-up, but she did believe that a serious mistake had been made that had caused all of the names to end up with the wrong people. And then these names had stuck, never to disappear or change. They stuck as firmly as the deep-black sweep of hair on Fathiya's head, as unchangingly as the certainty that Saada's curls would always fly wildly in whatever direction the wind was blowing.

It had been expected that the newborn would be celebrated in the usual festive manner as she completed her first week of life. Her sparse hair would be shaved off and weighed carefully and precisely, and that weight in silver would be gifted to the poor. Sweets would be handed out to the village children. The family would slaughter a goat or some other animal according to ritual and would parcel out the flesh among the folk of Sharaat Bat, this minute hamlet as invisible as its name suggested: tucked away just like an armpit, its squat little houses and slender irrigation canals like stray underarm hairs.

A festive occasion—had the village not been mourning her grandfather. The happy event could not take place now. The joy that normally greeted a birth did not find its way, not even partway, into the grieving heart of the baby's mother.

And so no one in Sharaat Bat was celebrating when Layla, or Ghazaala, reached the end of her first week. But on that very day in the capital city of Muscat, a festive occasion of a different sort occurred: the inaugural concert of the Royal Oman Symphony Orchestra. A boy of ten—a few years later he would be a violinist in that very orchestra—was following every moment of the concert on the television screen, dazzled by what he saw. He was in his family's run-down home in the old Muscat neighborhood of al-Hamriya. Never in his life had the boy so much as touched a musical instrument. But with his eyes fixed on the televised concert, the boy had no trouble imagining himself into the picture, up there among the musicians. He nourished himself on this dream and it seemed to fill his whole life.

By the time he earned his diploma from the Associated Board of the Schools of Music in London and officially joined the chamber orchestra of the Royal Oman Symphony, the Violin Player had left behind the family home in al-Hamriya for a modern high-rise in the newer district of al-Khuwair. Ghazaala's family had moved to that very building when she was fifteen. They had left their home in Sharaat Bat to be inhabited by their uncle, who was half insane by now.

There are people in this world who can live without love. But Ghazaala was certainly not one of them. Aged sixteen, she fell in love with her neighbor, the chamber orchestra violin player. For him she detached herself from the very core of her being. Body and soul, she stripped herself of everything she was. As she saw it, she was leaving her earthly self behind to sail off to the place where his spirit hovered. The silken wrap around her soul burned away like a mere length of fabric, and whatever smoke arose from the flames of it spelled out nothing other than the letters of his name. If he so much as gave her a real look, she thought, surely that would leave her full with child. If all she had in life was one final wish that might be granted, it would be to have his love.

Ghazaala ran away from home and married him.

With his slender fingers and his dreamy personality, the Violin Player led her through the treacherous thickets of love. He taught her how to make herself near-transparent, like a gauzy fabric; to be as soft and clear as a song in the ecstatic music-making of love. He taught her how to vibrate with desire as if she were one of the strings on his violin. He led her there with insistent speed and yet with the most deliberate slowness, too. She found in herself a wild spark of fever that she had never known before. Now, she fancied, she had reached the furthest edges of desire. Only much, much later did Ghazaala come to understand that desire is nothing more or less than a bottomless well.

7

Within five years Ghazaala had given birth to twins, finished her secondary education, and entered the university. In her final year of study in the College of Economics, the Violin Player ran away from the house of marriage.

Zahwa

Blossom of Life

After Wad Maayuf extracted his sister Sarira from the house of her husband Sallum and killed Sallum's cow, Mahbuba—"the Beloved"—was the only cow left in the village who could give the folk of Sharaat Bat the butter and fermented milk that they needed.

Ghazaala and Asiya toddled and played between Mahbuba's legs even before Ghazaala could walk. As Ghazaala crawled, Asiya would tug Ghazaala's hands in an attempt to hasten the moment when she would be able to stand up on her own. They were only a little older when they learned how to feed grass to the cow, slowly and patiently. They also tried to get Mahbuba to lick a strawberry lollipop and to munch on potato chips. One time they tried to pierce one of her ears with a metal poker because they had a silver earring that they wanted her to wear. If they could make that happen, then Mahbuba would look just like the cow with the earring they saw pictured on cheese packets. But Saada got to her cow just in time, sparing Mahbuba this catastrophe and sparing the little girls the cow's inevitable rage.

As they played around and beneath her, Mahbuba seemed to the two little girls to be an enormous and splendid creature. They never really caught on (or at least, not until long after their early girlhood) that she was actually a skinny, sallow heifer who looked nothing like the laughing cows in the cheese packets' colorful ads—nor did she resemble, in any way, the plump white cows that always followed Heidi so obligingly in the cartoon. But Mahbuba's emaciated figure in no way prevented her from producing the bounty that was hers to give. It was a familiar sight: the little girls of the village coming with their pails, gathering at Saada's in the high morning to fill up those pails with the buttermilk that would become the liquid in which bubbled the rice that was their main meal of the day. One might also see a peasant or a laborer of some sort stopping by very early in the morning to fill his metal cup with Mahbuba's milk. On some days the women of the neighborhood would send Saada their small, shallow bowls to fill with clarified butter made from Mahbuba's frothy cream.

Saada always woke up as the milking-star was appearing in the sky. That cows' star was her sign; it was time to get up. She would milk Mahbuba and prepare the animal's maghbara. To make it, she shredded clover into a large tin container, mixed in some sardines, and poured enough water over the mixture to make it slightly soupy. She lit a fire, and as the mixture heated she stirred and pounded it with her ladle, carved from the trunk of a date palm. Now it was ready, Mahbuba's feed. But after Wad Maayuf killed Sallum's cow (who had never had a name), Mahbuba refused to eat anything. She would not touch the maghbara. The situation got so desperate that Saada began asking herself seriously whether Mahbuba really did understand that her only companion in Sharaat Bat had been slain. Ghazaala and Asiya were too small to comprehend what had happened— although the news had reached them with the dawn, along with everyone else in every home in the village.

Sarira had burned Sallum's loaf of bread. His response was to fix the burned bread prominently to the front door of their home with a nail he pounded into the wood. He wanted everyone to see what a disgrace this woman was. His act made Sarira angry and she picked a quarrel with her husband. She knew how to give the disagreement a sharp edge by raising, at just the right moment, the shame-causing subject of his unknown origins. Sallum stalked out of the house. By the time he came back it was far into the night and Sarira had gone to sleep. He undid the end of the rope tied to the stake, leaving the other end laced as it was through his cow's mouth and around her head. As quickly as he could, he carried the free rope end inside and bound up his slumbering wife's hands with it and he gave the cow a light slap. This was the cow's usual signal: it was time to trot to Sallum's field on the other side of the village. But this time she was dragging Sarira behind her. The woman was barefoot and bareheaded. Struck dumb by the terror of this sudden shock coming in the midst of her deep sleep, she was completely incapable of stopping the cow from making its eager way toward the field.

By the time Saada was treating Sarira's wounds with red gum sap drawn from a dragon's-blood tree and lathering Sarira's blistered hands with a preparation made from pounded milk thistle, Sarira's brother Wad Maayuf had killed the cow. When morning came, the children gathered to stare at the carcass. Flies circled overhead. In a piercingly high voice Asiya asked, "Why doesn't this cow have a name?" No one answered her question. She took Ghazaala, who was crying, by the hand and they walked to the falaj. There at the edge of the irrigation channel, Asiya took off her gown, keeping on the slip she wore underneath. She helped Ghazaala take off her gown. She rinsed the younger girl's face, trying to remove the traces of tears and snot that had been triggered at the sight of blood pooled beneath the cow. They jumped into the flowing water and raced each other against the current, chasing after the little black fish and the treacherous water snakes. Cautiously they entered the narrower covered shafts branching off the falaj's main canal, navigating them expertly until they came out once again into the wider uncovered channel. So absorbed were they in their play that they momentarily forgot that some of the smaller underground shafts of the falaj system opened straight into village households. Suddenly, at Fadiya's house two little heads appeared. Fadiya was older than Asiya and Ghazaala. She had already started school and sometimes, these days, she wouldn't even play with them. She always said that she had something called "homework" to do. But at the sight of them popping up in the falaj opening, Fadiya collapsed into laughter. She immediately stripped off her outer chemise, keeping on her undershirt and sirwal, and jumped into the water alongside them. She led the two smaller girls, swimming across the covered canals that led away from the houses and into the main waterway where they'd started. Then the girls lay in the sunshine, their bodies turned toward the heights nearby, to dry themselves off. They got dressed. Holding her head very high Fadiya said, "I have some math homework to do." She scurried home.

Asiya and Ghazaala returned to the house. They gulped down the soft, spongy coconut sweet that Saada's hands had shaped and sat in front of the television to watch *Heidi*. When Fathiya appeared as the sun was about to go down, the littler girl started crying as she always did. Ghazaala didn't want to go home. She clutched at Asiya's clothing. She wouldn't let go until Saada promised she would come and get her early in the morning so that she could help Saada milk Mahbuba.

But the next morning was the first Friday of the month—and as always, this meant there would be some little family festivities at Saada's. Her husband would be coming home. He worked for the Emirates military in Abu Dhabi City. Whenever he came home to Sharaat Bat he was always carrying cartons of oranges, apples, and bananas, bags of sweets, balloons, and dolls for his only daughter. The house filled with the scent of frankincense and the sounds of joy. Mother and daughter hovered around their husband and father as he spun stories of the latest month he had spent working for the army and away from his family.

When morning came and there was no sign of Saada, Ghazaala slipped out of the house on her own. Her mother was still asleep. Her uncle was bent over bits of electric wire and electronic components that he was untangling and taking apart. Her aunt Maliha's attention was focused on her coffee and her plate of dates. Panting hard, Ghazaala reached Asiya's house. She stopped and stood in front of the open gate into the courtyard. She could see Saada sitting on an empty overturned Nido dried-milk can, undoing her wet hair and at the same time baking thin loaves of bread on the hot tin surface in the courtyard. She was singing.

> Her graceful walk, her henna tracings
> How lovely her ring the day it sparkles on
> her finger

I swore I would craft her an earring and two
   dinar drops
One of them mushammas and the other,
   Bahraini
One is worth four thousand and one, two
   thousand!

Ghazaala forgot how annoyed she had been feeling. She walked in and crouched next to Saada. "Mama Saada," she said, "give me some hot bread, but please will you sprinkle it with samna and sugar first." Ghazaala's own father came home once a month, or sometimes twice. He worked in the Ministry of Housing in Muscat. But their house never smelled of incense and it was never full of dolls and sweets for her and the other children. Her mother never sang beautiful songs the way Saada did.

It would have seemed so ordinary, so natural, for Saada to live to be a hundred years old. For Saada to always be there, preparing maghbara for the cow and coconut sweets for the children, drawing milk and cream, feeding Ghazaala and Asiya and Mahbuba and the goats, undoing her hair and baking as she sang, exuding a fragrance of incense and fresh dough, laughing her ringing laugh, and forever gathering the plants that could treat poisons and fevers from the high slopes surrounding Sharaat Bat. So natural for Saada to continue nursing babies who had been flung into the air and away from their own mothers' milk, even as an old woman with a face full of wrinkles. But Saada never made it, not even to thirty. She died one year after the death of her second daughter, Zahwa, the Blossom of Life.

The sign at the entrance to the narrow dirt lane leading into Sharaat Bat, the armpit village tucked away inside the hills—the sign saying SHARAAT BAT in white letters on a blue background—was taken down the year Asiya and Ghazaala started school. Work began on an asphalt road that was to replace the village's packed-dirt street, and soon a new sign was there, its blue deeper and the white thicker and brighter than the old. But what was written on it was something entirely new. AL-WAHA. The Oasis.

It was the calamitous event of going to school that occupied the girls rather than the new presence of construction workers or the new sign. Now, instead of scampering behind Saada on the elevations near the village to gather plants, or rolling down the shorter slopes, or forcing the cat, Shaybub, to take a bath with them in the falaj, or teasing the donkey, Naazi', "Mr. Troublesome," and pelting him with pebbles, or racing the boys, or hunting sparrows with bows and arrows, or stealing ripe mangoes from the fields, or looking for the chocolate that Aunt Maliha had hidden somewhere in her room, suddenly here they were. Here, sitting in a crowded little room in a pale yellowish building at the village limits. They could hear the bulldozers' roar—paving the new road—all the while that Abla Iffat (who was terribly tall and big and carried a whip and had a strange way of speaking because she was not from around here) made them sit still and stay quiet.

Almost instantaneously Miss Iffat got very cross with the two of them. Asiya should have started school the year before, but she had waited for Ghazaala so that they could start together. Then, this teacher from Egypt—this woman they had to call Abla Iffat—lost her self-control altogether and began screaming at them. "Ya ghagar! You gypsy children, you are mad!" That was because the teacher had been caught unawares as she found herself under attack from sharp fingernails and teeth. Asiya's assault was accompanied by a loud and steady screech issuing from Ghazaala. Abla Iffat had tried to separate them. Her intention was to put Ghazaala in the first row because she was so small and Asiya in the back row since she was tall for her age. Her action led instead to a pitched battle, as most of the other pupils jumped in. The authorities were summoned—the mothers, since the fathers were always at a distant workplace. The two little girls were made to apologize to Abla Iffat. And then they were seated together in the middle row.

What made school even more terrifying was the trip home in the afternoon, when one of the Indian road-construction workers was lying in wait for the girls. He appeared suddenly in a deserted spot and made strange movements that they didn't understand. Then he peed in front of them and vanished. They fled, Ghazaala squeezing Asiya's hand in fright as she asked, over and over, "Why does his pee look different? Why does he make us watch him? Is he going to hit us next time?" Asiya didn't have any answers to give. The mystifying performance occurred several times and then Asiya filled her pinafore pockets with sharp stones, reluctant to leave the school building until she felt confident that she had a heavy enough load of them. But she had to wait a week before the man appeared again. She shivered at the sight of his red-squared kerchief. But calmly she shoved Ghazaala behind her and began pitching stones at him. Then she ran off, towing Ghazaala behind her, the two of them moving as fast as they could. After that day the construction worker with the odd-looking pee did not appear again.

Asiya and Ghazaala headed straight to Suhayb's shop, making a great deal of racket as they did so. They had in mind a bag of Chips Oman. Once they were at home, they would dip the potato chips into buttermilk and wolf them down. As they burst in noisily, Suhayb bolted up from his seat. He had popped a tape into the player. As he listened, he was completely riveted by the image on the cassette box— Nagat al-Saghira, the Egyptian singer and film star, indeed the Egyptian heartthrob. Aunt Maliha was close behind the two girls. She glanced narrowly at Nagat's image with obvious disdain.

"My uncle and his friends always sat together for this kind of thing—and it wasn't just to *listen* to Samira Tawfiq. What they really wanted was to stare at the famous black mole on her face. Looks like the new generation of boys are still having their little fantasies about singers."

Clearly Suhayb was flustered. His face went bright red at Maliha's insinuation. Maliha was no older than he was but she always acted as though she were his senior. Maliha might be hanging up posters of Mustafa Qamar and Raghib Allama inside her wardrobe, but she could ridicule those celebrity ad spots from the nineties that told people what they ought to eat and what they should be drinking and how to dress. For Suhayb she had one remark: "Dancing to real music is one thing—it's an art. But dancing to a tune advertising a bottle of cooking oil is a completely different matter."

Suhayb had been meaning to broadcast one of the music ads for Super Jameel nappies in his shop. Surely, their lively song and dance would be a draw. But now he was embarrassed. He could see already that this woman wouldn't take kindly to such a move. Anyway, at least Aunt Maliha bought a whole carton of Chips Oman before she turned to leave Suhayb's shop.

As Ghazaala was trotting out of the shop, though, she called loudly after her aunt. "We aren't going to buy anything from your little shop! We'll buy at Suhayb's." Her aunt gave her a piece of her mind and turned back to Suhayb. "I don't have a *shop*, you know," she said. "It's just that sometimes, when the little ones are all running around out there just in front of the house, I sell them a few bags of Chips Oman and some candy. By the way, Suhayb—those spots for Chips Oman, I don't like them at all. This girl with bright yellow hair holding on tight to her bag of potato chips and singing 'chips from Oman.' 'From *Ooamaaan*,' she wails—just listen to her go on and on! It's written right there on the packet, where they're from, where else would they be from?"

Suhayb laughed and Maliha's face softened. She knew very well that when evening came Suhayb would shut off the power to the fridge in the shop because he dreaded a spike in his next electricity bill. But then the village mothers would come to him clutching cartons of milk and angrily waving them at him, because they had gone sour long before the use-by date. Suhayb always denied vehemently that he shut off the electricity at night. He didn't consider the milk spoilage—or the ice cream that was only frozen hard at the sides of the container and not at the center because it didn't refreeze properly— as sufficient proof to justify their accusation. Maliha never shut off the little fridge in her room. But she didn't load it up, either—not with anything more than a few cartons of juice and some ice cream cones. She never sold milk. She really had no intention of competing with Suhayb.

Maliha stowed the carton of Chips Oman away under her bed and sat down to riffle through a magazine. She had learned how to read and write, and do some basic arithmetic, from Salima, the Qur'an-school teacher. She avidly followed two magazines from the Gulf, *Sayyidati* and *Zahrat al-Khalij*, which reached the village because Asiya's father brought them from town for his wife, Saada. At some point Maliha wrote her first letter to *Sayyidati*. She wanted to comment on a particular regular column.

Dear Editor of "Your Problem Has a Solution":

Well, my problem is that our house is ancient and has no modern furnishings at all. All we have are cushions and mats. We don't have any of your striped sofas, none of those elegant yellow easy chairs that you see in the TV serial *Kharag wa lam ya'ud*.

Best wishes,
Your devoted sister Maliha,
from al-Waha

Absorbed in her magazine on this particular day, Maliha remembered suddenly that Saada was in the hospital. She hardly had time to ask herself what the two girls might be doing right now, when she heard Ghazaala shouting.

"I'm going to the hospital with Asiya, Aunt! Tell my mother."

Saada had had another stillbirth. The doctors said they didn't know why. There was no heartbeat, they told her, and she would need to have curettage, her uterus scraped. Her husband loaded the car with cartons of oranges, apples, and bananas, boxes of dates, and thermoses of coffee. He took Asiya and Ghazaala with him to the central hospital in Sur City. In the broad open space in front of the hospital he spread out a blanket and arranged all of the treats he had brought with them. When anyone came in or out he called them over for coffee and fruit—a host's generous offering for the sake of Saada's health. After the hospital security men began harassing him, he waved to the knot of Bedouin huddling nearby to come and join him instead in the empty lot behind the hospital, where he spread out his welcome blanket once again.

Ghazaala and Asiya got involved in some games that other children were playing in the hospital yard. When visiting hours began and the doors opened, the guard prevented the children from going in and Ghazaala started crying. Asiya's father gave her a wink and she quieted down, huddling with her milk-sister on one of the metal benches outside the hospital where they would wait for him. The promise in his eyes told them that they would get to see Mama Saada.

As Asiya's father was coming out of the building, the girls were again playing a familiar game with some children in front of the hospital entrance. He could hear their sing-song chant, "Open up, little flower! Close now, flower!" They ran over to him. Giving them a sign to quiet down, he led them in silence along the hospital wall and turned a corner, still following closely along the external wall parallel to the windows of the ward where overnight patients slept. Asiya's father slowed his pace, paused in hesitation, walked past several more windows and began to call out in a very low voice, "Saada . . . Saada." They all edged forward, but then stepped back a bit, unsure, before a particular window opened. Sticking out between two metal bars, Saada's hand was waving. "Mama!" the two girls exclaimed at once.

Somehow, Asiya's father fetched a wooden stool with a broken leg. He propped it up with two stout tree branches. Standing on it, the girls could see their mother. When they got tired of balancing on this precarious perch, he seated himself on the stool and pulled them onto his lap. The evening passed with the four of them chattering. Though she was very weak, Saada was laughing. The two girls were ecstatic at the success of this revenge against the guard who had barked at them, "Children are not allowed inside!" It grew late and the girls fell asleep in Asiya's father's arms. He said his goodbyes to Saada and led the girls back to the car. On the way home Ghazaala opened her eyes suddenly. "Ummi Saada is pretty, isn't she?" she said to him.

Her words startled him. He laughed. "Your mama Saada is pretty, yes she is . . . but even if she weren't, I . . ." He found it hard to go on, unaccustomed to speaking of such matters. He couldn't find the right words. He just laughed again, embarrassed, and then he tried to go on. "I never get tired of her." His face lit up, as if these were precisely the words he had meant to say. He said them again. "I don't grow tired of her, I never feel bored with your mama Saada."

Before summer came and the school year ended, Saada gave birth to her second daughter, Zahwa. After two miscarriages, the successful arrival of this newborn elated her. Her husband took a week off from work. There were joyful visits and celebratory gatherings. Platters of the traditional warm, dark, jellylike Omani sweet dotted with almonds were passed around. There were fancy little glasses of frankincense-scented water and baskets of fruit waiting for all of those who came to congratulate the new mother.

A few months of life, and this beautiful child with her delicate features had captivated her parents completely. Her father now came home from Abu Dhabi more than once a month so that he wouldn't miss Zahwa's new babblings as she learned to talk, or the first time she sat up on her own, or when she began to crawl. But he had to wait two years before she was walking on those little feet, which her mama had coated with henna. By this time Saada almost never left the house or the area around it. She was hardly attending to Mahbuba or the goats because she spent the entirety of her days caring for Zahwa—bathing her, nursing her, singing to her, sewing the most beautiful tiny gowns imaginable for this child who was the loveliest little creature she had ever set eyes on in her life.

When Old Raaya rapped on the door, Asiya opened it. Saada's voice could be heard from inside the house, happy and vigorous, as she bounced Zahwa to the rhythm of her chant. "Ba'jin wa-baghrif wa-batlaa fil-ghuraf . . . I knead and I ladle and I climb to the higher rooms."

"How is your mother?" Raaya asked the older daughter. Asiya spun her finger at her own head. Cuckoo! Raaya laughed. "That gorgeous little wonder, the blooming Zahwa, well, she deserves a little madness and some crazy talk. But . . . do you have any rice around here?"

Asiya went into the kitchen. She filled a small plastic sack with rice and came out and handed it to Raaya. Everyone knew that this woman no longer had any need to go around begging, but they also understood that it had become a habit with her. Raaya had five sons who were all government employees in Muscat. They took good care of her; they didn't spare any expense. Everyone knew that she stowed large sacks of rice and packets of tea and coffee and sugar and powdered milk underneath her wooden bedframe. And that she still spent her days making her rounds and asking folks for food.

At Sarira's wedding to her second husband, Tahir—she had agreed to marry him strictly on condition, formally agreed, that he would never own a cow, never in his life and not for any reason he might give, or argument he might make, whatsoever—Raaya got into a quarrel with the bridegroom. He had noticed her filching meat. She was packing it away in a large clay pot to take home. Tahir scolded her in front of everyone, embarrassing her to the point that her skinny figure was a mass of tremors and she looked about to collapse into sobs and tears. If a body didn't see any mercy or any charity from her own town folk, she moaned, then where would she find it? From that day on, the folk of Sharaat Bat—or now, al-Waha—had nothing to say about Raaya. Without comment they gave her what she asked for. Asiya in particular liked to give Raaya whatever she wanted. That was because Asiya enjoyed visiting Raaya at home and scooting around playfully amid the bags of sugar and the enormous sacks of flour, pretending as she wrapped Raaya's shawl around her head like a turban that she was the chief merchant lady of the market. She would summon the other children to bargain with her over buying this or that pile of cracked wheat or rice, or jars of pickled vegetables. One time the children succeeded in fooling the old woman and loading up Naazi' the donkey with a cooking pot and two large sacks of raw chickpeas. They led the animal away and got as far as the base of the mountains, a spot just before you would have to start climbing. They built a campfire and cooked the chickpeas and ate them all, very quickly, even though the beans were only half cooked and completely unsalted.

Asiya came home late in the afternoon with her tummy aching. Her mother motioned at her fiercely to keep quiet so that she wouldn't wake the tiny girl, who had just gone to sleep. Asiya was expecting a scolding for coming home so late. But Saada didn't say anything about that. She just kept humming softly to the baby. Asiya went outside again and walked to Ghazaala's house. Auntie Maliha brought her back after the evening meal. She stood still in the doorway. Her mother was tickling Zahwa and teasing her. "How good you look! Shall I eat you up? Eat you uppah, heh?" Asiya whispered, "Yes, eat her up, just eat her all up," and went off to bed.

Zahwa must have toppled into the falaj around midday. It was so hot at that hour that rarely did anyone leave their house. Most people were napping. No one was likely to be using the irrigation channels for anything at that time. The current, in its onrush from one orchard to the next, would have carried her from one branch of the canal system to the next. Finally, the pressure of the moving water must have wedged her against one of the strong wooden blocks in the sluice that directed a measured flow of water out to irrigate a particular orchard at a particular time. Zahwa drowned.

No one made an effort to revive her because when they found her, it was clear from the bloated body that she had been dead for hours. They carried the small body—which hadn't even experienced three full years of life—and they laid it in Saada's arms. The short wet locks of hair dampened Saada's lap as she began squeezing water out of the cloth amulets her daughter wore; the fabric was soaked. She hugged the little body tightly and begged—by God's ultimate truth, by the glory of the Prophet, by the greatness of all the prophets and the holy presence of the sainted, by the Companions of the Prophet, by the martyrs and the pious—that her daughter might wake up. Sitting cross-legged on the ground, her arms wrapped tightly around the wet little body, she whispered, "Get up, Zahwa, get up, up, my Zahwa, Zahwati, get up, wake up, c'mon, Maah, wake up." The women pried the body away from Saada's chest and ordered her to say other words. "Say: We are all God's creatures and to God we return." Saada smeared dirt all over her head and rubbed it into her hair and her face. She would never be the same woman again.

The bereaved mother ran into the courtyard of her home and pored over the footprints of her little one, still pressed into the muddy ground around the bushes and small trees in the courtyard space. She spread her hands over the footprints, bewildered. She hurried away to fetch a stack of ceramic bowls that she had kept; these bowls had held the sweets made specifically for the festive meals that followed

Zahwa's birth. She overturned them onto the mud, covering the traces of those little footprints one by one, with every bowl. She wanted desperately to preserve these footprints from erasure for as long as she could.

Less than a month had passed since Zahwa's burial, when Saada gripped a large, thick nail and scratched words onto the metal door to her home. Saada sinner Saada sinner Saada sinner. SAADA AYBA SAADA AYBA SAADA AYBA. The neighborhood women chided her for it, but she wouldn't listen to any of their cautions. She was culpable; she was the sinner because she had fallen asleep forgetting that the door was unlatched. She was the one who had left her child to wander off and to run, to drown, to die in the irrigation sluice on a blazing midday. She was AYBA and she would maintain that word there, carving it over and over into the door of her house so that everyone would know the wrong she had done. The women told her it was destiny. But Saada only retraced the words on the door with her nail to etch them more deeply into the metal. When children die, the women said, they go straight to heaven. But Saada shut her door in their faces, her sin scratched indelibly onto it, and she shut herself in. The neighborhood women murmured that with the girl's death, the mother had lost her mind. They shook their heads and muttered, "All might and all power are God's alone."

When, soon after, the Emirates military demobilized the thousands of Omanis in their employ, the officer in mourning returned home permanently—returned to Zahwa's grave and his wife's state of utter wreckage and despair. Surely, he thought, if he gave her a new child her zest for life would return. But Saada wouldn't let him touch her. Her eyes wide open in an unmoving stare, she would not budge from where she lay on the flat roof, no longer able to do anything. He sold Mahbuba and the goats. Now he made Saada's meals, preparing them carefully, pureeing everything as if it were baby food, because she wouldn't chew anything that he put in her mouth. She just swallowed immediately. He bathed her and pressed her clothes and kept the house clean, all the while hoping desperately that she would come out of her extreme grief and return to him and to Asiya. But she had sunk into depths beyond them and she stayed there until her death.

Saada was buried next to Zahwa, and her husband submerged himself in drink. At first, this was a matter of top-quality bottles sent to him by his old friends from the army, wrapped up with care and lined up tightly in wooden orange crates. But then he had to resort to buying cans of beer on the black market. When his money ran out he began getting high on cheap cologne, glue, paint fumes, and shoe polish. Sitting in front of the house, he didn't try to hide his intoxicated state from anyone. When he collapsed, Asiya and Ghazaala would drag him inside and spray him off with the hose to clean off the residues of vomit.

Fadiya would no longer speak to Asiya, because her father

was a dissolute. Raaya the beggar woman wouldn't let Asiya inside her house to borrow a bit of rice or flour from the big burlap sacks crammed under the bed whose use-by date had long since passed. Moreover, Asiya and Ghazaala were now too old to swim in the falaj channels or run races with the other village children as they had done when they were little. The only way they could pass the time was by taking long, silent walks through the orchards.

Lining up for school each morning, they could see the teacher staring at Asiya. She would declare that the presence of perverted people with their wicked habits in the village endangered everyone. Aged fourteen, Asiya left school. At home, she gathered all her belongings and locked the mandus lid over the clothing of her dead sister and her dead mother. That big wooden chest with its few contents had been everything her mother brought to her marriage. Asiya left the mandus where it sat in the house and led her drunk father outside by the hand. She was carrying her schoolbag. She had dumped out the books and filled it instead with the few items she possessed. She locked the metal door—the years had not softened the words that Saada had scratched there. With her father, Asiya left Shaarat Bat and never came back. The neighborhood women said she had gone to her maternal uncles in al-Waafi. Others were certain that she had taken her father back to his old home in Abu Dhabi and that the two of them had opened a shop there. But no one actually heard any news of where she was or what she was doing. She never returned to her mother's locked mandus in the closed-up house. But years later, her voice could be heard across the airwaves and TV speakers.

21 November 2006

At about nine o'clock every evening I have to abandon my lecture notebooks and research materials, or the metal dinner plates in the residence hall's cafeteria if I'm still having dinner, or my phone conversation with Mama, or our informal races around the quad. I have to get myself quickly over to the office of the supervisor of this residential block to register that I am here. Every night. I have to establish— along with thousands of other students, all of the women who live here—that we are in for the night here in the university residence.

A week ago, during our 10:00 a.m. lecture, Ghazaala passed me a note inviting me to her boys' birthday party. When I lifted my head after reading it I saw that the lecturer was staring at me. Why does someone as full of himself as this man pay attention to such trivial business? We had already nicknamed him Genghis Khan because he was such a tyrant. Once he shifted his gaze away from me, I gave Ghazaala a little wave to say yes, even though I didn't have the slightest idea of how to leave university housing without special permission. But I don't like to pass up anything that has to do with Ghazaala. That's been true ever since our first year, from the day she fell asleep in a math lecture. When the professor asked her, "What's this? Didn't you sleep last night?" she answered immediately with a short sharp sentence of her own. "I was cleaning out the fridge." That's the moment when I made up my mind that she would become my friend.

After signing in at 9:00 p.m. and attending a discussion section for my research group on the basics of marketing, I went to my room thinking only of sleep. But my roommate, Shuruq, was sitting there. Normally we don't have much to say to each other; Shuruq considers me someone she must "disassociate from" because I don't behave or believe properly. And that means it wouldn't do for her to show me any affection. But this evening, she asked me whether I was planning to attend tomorrow's lecture by the famous Iraqi British preacher in the large conference lecture hall. I shook my head. Then she shook her head, but more slowly, to show how sorry she was that I wouldn't be going. Her schemes to persuade me to her side have been obvious failures, but she still never misses a chance to make it clear that she's unhappy with me disobeying her directives. I've heard that many of the students here selected their roommates, but I am not one of them. Anyway, at the time I didn't have any close friends I could choose from. And Ghazaala was living with her husband quite far away from the university.

The girl who lives in the room on the floor above, just over ours, dresses like Shuruq. She wears a long abaya, draped over her head and pinned into place, with black stockings. She has never said a word. I haven't seen her show any interest in lecturing a student whose hair is visible or whose phone can be heard playing music. She hasn't accosted any girls in the big courtyard onto which our university residence halls open, ordering them to wear long coats, even in this sheltered space, because male workers are sometimes around. Like Shuruq does. I've never seen that girl giving anyone advice about attending the once-a-week religious lectures. And she always walks as if she is following a perfectly straight line. She did pause to stare at me and my classmates when we were racing each other around the large courtyard. But then she just went on, along that imaginary straight line. Always alone, perfectly self-sufficient I guess, not wanting anyone's attention—as though her world is completely an internal one and she doesn't have any need of the world we're living in. One evening I heard some strange sounds coming through her window, like the moans and gurgles of an animal whose throat has just been slit. When I came inside and finally decided that I ought to go upstairs and investigate, I found her door open as if she had just left the room.

Maybe to the bathroom? I couldn't resist going into her room. The long vertical mirror above the washbasin was covered entirely by brown paper, the kind people use as protective wrapping over their book covers. The curtain was partway open and I could see that the window was covered completely in newspaper pages. No posters, no pictures, no papers or even books on the desk. Water was dripping from the washbasin tap. Before I went out—wanting to be quick about it—I couldn't help looking again at the faded brown paper over the mirror. Exactly at the center I noticed the little photo of a small child who couldn't have been older than three.

But I heard footsteps in the corridor so I didn't linger. In the dining hall I slid my metal tray down the long table until it was next to a tray piled with fried chicken legs. Salaayim's favorite meal. I pulled out the chair next to her and sat down. She gave me a skeptical look, so I started the conversation. "How are you, Salaayim? I haven't seen you for a while." It only took her a minute to decide that this was good enough, and she started talking. Salaayim is the greatest gossip this residence hall has known—I'm sure of that. Her small eyes start flashing whenever she hears a fresh piece of news about anyone. Her face glows as she makes a big show of lowering her voice to pass on whatever bit of tittle-tattle she has. She knows everything about everybody: The second-year student who escaped one weekend with a male student from the same year, only to be nabbed by the police as they were returning through the main gate. Or the prof in the College of Agriculture who gave his students answers before an exam so they would write him glowing reviews and his contract wouldn't be canceled. The dean who was inviting the classiest male students—only first-years, though—to come have a swim together in the big pool on his farm. The student in sciences who committed suicide after she got a warning that she would be expelled permanently from the university because she was failing academically. The young women in the College of Arts who punctured the tires of the car belonging to the professor of modern criticism. The father who came to the residence hall and dragged his daughter out by her hair as everyone was watching. The prof in the business school who married his master's student when he already had a wife. Every piece of news, no matter how large or small, can be found with Salaayim. It's become the center of her life, I think. Salaayim herself has no story. The news about everybody else has stripped her of her own.

I tried to shift the conversation to our own particular residence hall. "Salaayim, don't you think there are some strange girls up on the third floor?" She laughed and curled her lips, which were greasy from the chicken. "Are there any girls who aren't strange?" In the end, I was forced into asking a direct question about the girl who was always alone and always silent and wore the abaya pinned to her head. Salaayim said she didn't know her, and in fact—and I was amazed to hear this!—she had never even tried to see the inside of her room. She shifted quickly to a different topic, chatting about her neighbor who slept on the floor and never on her bed and never ever flushed the toilet in the common bathroom.

I asked Shuruq about her, too. Shuruq just shrugged. "Don't let appearances deceive you. I've never seen her in the religion classes at the mosque. I keep close tabs on who goes regularly and who stays away. Even though this girl looks modest and devout, she's never come to one of those lessons."

This person who covers her mirror and her window has begun to obsess me. I have followed her, almost tailed her, through the corridors on the third floor and down the stairs and into the inner courtyard of our block of residences. I can pick up her scent. The smell of a wild animal, or maybe of wild plants; more like fruit than flowers. I always maintain a distance between us. But even at a distance I can see her hands clearly, sticking out of the sleeves of her black abaya. Big hands for a young woman. No rings or bangles, and her fingers seem to clench up and then unfurl suddenly as if she can't control the way they move. Her walk isn't particularly fast but it isn't slow, either. She's always wearing black flats when I've seen her. Once or twice I've said hello to her. She looked at me for a moment and then gave me a slight nod. This person does not seem interested in words or in having anyone's company. I have never seen her when she isn't alone.

I've never caught a glimpse of her in the dining hall or in the matron's office at the hour we are supposed to show up and sign in. I have hardly ever heard her voice.

When I was in my first year of university and I heard Ghazaala tell the professor that she hadn't slept because she'd been cleaning out the refrigerator, I went straight over to her after the lecture. "My name is Harir. I'm from Sohar and I want to be your friend."

Ghazaala laughed and shook my hand. She was clearly a bit startled. If only I had the same kind of courage now that I had then, I've thought sometimes. If only I could put myself squarely in the path of this strange young woman and say to her, "Be my friend." But I hadn't even dared to look directly into her face; though if I did, I wouldn't be able to see anything beyond her eyes—the look in her eyes. I'm imagining that she has studied all the possible expressions a person's eyes can hold, as if she has seen them all on display in front of her, and she decided this blank blind stare was the one for her. She put it on like one would a garment. It's a look that sees but can't be seen. A look that says to the world: Everything I see looks alike and nothing I see changes anything inside of me. This look, this expression that has held me prisoner, has made me follow this girl who covers her mirror and sticks the photo of a little girl at the center of all that brown paper. That little child who could be her or someone very like her.

Two days after this, Salaayim gave me a little tap on the shoulder. "Harir, the girl on the third floor—she's in the College of Education, and no one lives in that room with her." There was a triumphant tone in Salaayim's voice. Suddenly an idea bolted through my mind. What if I were to come forward and ask to share her room? The classmate who was with Salaayim shrugged her shoulders as she stirred milk into her Nescafé and insisted she had seen the same student carrying a white overcoat over her arm. That meant she must be in the College of Medicine or somewhere in the sciences. "Maybe she's in her third year, like me," I said. Salaayim shook her head. She hadn't seen her in the residence hall in the previous two years. Hadn't seen her at all until this year.

Then Salaayim lost interest in checking out the mysterious girl and began—in rapid-fire words, as if she had to get it all out in one single breath—telling the story of the professor from Cyprus in the Language Center who adopted a camel. She imitated the instructor, trying to keep from laughing so hard she wouldn't be able to finish. "It's a genuine camel, boys, the real thing. I pay something every month to a Bedouin family over in Wahiba Sands to take care of it. The poor thing—I do go out there every week to visit it."

As I resumed walking, Salaayim followed close behind me. "And have you heard about the camel keeper's friend? Professor David? It's clear he doesn't have any kind of diploma, he's just kind of a chancer. Seems he was a comedy

44

actor in New Zealand. When he failed at that he opened a restaurant. Then he drove livestock trucks. But he went broke so he decided to come here and teach us his mother tongue. Just like that, no diploma. And their colleague from South Africa—the minute she comes into the lecture hall and sits down, she opens her briefcase and takes out a whole lot of chocolates, every brand you can buy. She lines them up on the desk in front of her and then she begins the class. When it's over she sweeps them all back into her bag and leaves the room"—here I had to break in. "I have to go and sign in with the matron. See you later, Salaayim."

On Thursday Ghazaala picked me up after lectures were done. I crouched on the back-seat floor as we passed the university police at the main gate, since I didn't have a permission slip to leave campus. When we came back after her boys' party, she dropped me off in front of the residence hall and I went straight to the office to sign in before going to my room. I found Shuruq there listening to a lecture. I was exhausted and collapsed onto the chair. The lecturer was talking about the breakup of the family unit. Things are so bad, he exclaimed, that husbands and wives have their own keys to the house. I asked Shuruq whether the views of this lecturer were based on some sort of religious opinion or did it have to do with social strata where no one could imagine a woman having possession of a key to her own house. Shuruq got annoyed with me. This sort of thinking, she snapped, debased our respect for the preacher. The Fates willed that not long after my exchange with Shuruq this preacher was imprisoned following a harassment case.

I closed my eyes and tried to go to sleep. But something was getting me down, weighing on me. It wasn't what Shuruq said. These kinds of discussions with her always happen and they are a lost cause anyway. What kind of dialogue is it when, before you can even say a word, the other person already believes that they have the absolute truth and you are wrong by definition, no matter what you say? And that they are right already, whatever it is they are disputing. There's no real discussion to be had as long as they say they are speaking on the authority of the religion, or what they think the religion is. And you're just standing there powerless, deprived of any such monumental authority as this.

No, it wasn't that exchange with Shuruq that has left me feeling low and sluggish. It was something else, something about the birthday party. Something about Ghazaala's husband. That orchestra musician. He was wearing a striped gray shirt and for the entire party he stood in one corner leaning against the wall as if he would vanish any second. He didn't speak to anybody. He didn't move from that one spot unless Ghazaala or one of the boys asked him for something. If a balloon popped he didn't even blink, and he didn't react when it all got a little noisier or the children started running and skipping around. As if his corner was a world completely disengaged from ours. He was looking at us but he wasn't seeing us. We sang but he didn't hear us. We opened gifts amid the shouts of the children; at that point, he had a sort of little smile on his face and a look of slight indulgence. He hardly said a word, as if his fragile build and silence could shrink and set apart the space he occupied in the world. As if he wasn't really there. Or as if his being there was something one couldn't hold on to or even be certain about.

The Singer to the Queen

The Singer to the Queen said: "Ghazaala, O Gazelle—Your Majesty, does it make any sense that a queen of your stature would come from a village that bears this very strange name? Sharaat Bat? Armpit Hairs?"

He began laughing—the laughter that means peace and welcome, the laughter that brings healing, the laughter of respite.

She repeated: "I told you, its name changed the year I started school. Orders came down from on high to change it to al-Waha."

"Yes, that's right. Oasis—an oasis among the mountains."

"And—Sharaat Bat was not misnamed. Picture these high mountains. The only passage they allow into the village is a narrow wadi that cuts between two mountains. When the waters are high, the roads are blocked. In the small area inside this ring of mountains a few houses are scattered here and there, and some orchards—and they are even more scattered. And the irrigation canal artery between them, bisecting the space, and smaller ones going into these spaces— these houses and orchards, they're like slightly stray hairs sprouting from the underarm of the earth."

He laughed. "Amazing. By God, just amazing."

She laughed, too, admitting it. "Sing that for me—Ajib wallah ajib . . ."

He began to sing and he kept on singing until she fell asleep. While still between sleep and wakefulness, she murmured her thanks to Facebook for having introduced her to the Singer to the Queen and for being made a queen.

The Singer to the Queen ushered her into the evening with the rituals of evening, and he abandoned her to the daytime so that she could perform the rituals of dailiness. The Singer to the Queen adored pampering her. But everything about *him* was strictly off-limits. Nothing there that could be touched. Not his voice; not his skin; not his shirt or the cup of tea they pretended they were having together. Not the wood panel on which he was executing his latest painting. Not the rustle of lace on the dress of his little daughter, so far away in her mother's arms in a remote land in which the faraway little girl did not speak Arabic.

He said he was a confirmed bachelor. He loved women whose only demand was to be sung to and pampered. Yes, he said, he had been married. Once, to the foreign woman who gave him the little girl. Then she took the little girl and, protected by the laws of foreigners, she fled. But freedom, he said, was more important than fatherhood itself. He said he missed the little girl who would become an older girl but would not know how to say *Father* in Arabic.

Now the daylight hours were dedicated to daylight people, and the evening hours belonged to the Singer to the Queen, who knew perfectly well that she was not a queen. He knew that she had been raised in Sharaat Bat and he knew she had a milk-sister whom she hadn't seen for many years. He knew that there were twins in tow, always tugging at her and seeing nothing in her except "my mother"—a mother outside of time or space, a mother without any other identity. It didn't matter whether she was young or old, abandoned or beloved, whether she could live without love or could not—she was a mother. She was not a human being but a role, a set of tasks. It didn't make any difference to the twins that the age difference between the two of them and their mama was only eighteen years. In the boys' heads she was Mother and that was that. And anyway, this was the only certain thing in her life now.

A Singer to a Queen is not concerned with what or how much he knows. He goes on singing to his queen as long and as loudly as he can. After all, a queen will not demand that they go out to have some fun or that they transform an imagined cup of tea into a real plate of food sitting in front of her.

She doesn't try to monitor her chorister's mail and she doesn't put his masculinity on trial with the sort of passion that demands touching and feeling. For she is the queen and she sits on a distant throne. She is exactly like the faraway little girl who stumbles over the words *my father* and who has never played with his paintbrushes and messed them up or walked barefoot over canvases that aren't yet dry. This was as close as one could get to being simply and only a voice—whether it was the little girl or whether it was Ghazaala. A faraway voice, a modest and amenable voice, one that is content with the songs she hears over the telephone and the fancy cards he makes—especially for her, he makes them!—and sends to her on time, to celebrate holidays.

The Singer to the Queen alighted in Ghazaala's life two years after the Violin Player departed from it. His throat was the golden cave in which she could dwell, protected from the stings of the Violin Player's flight from her. When he sang to her his voice dislodged the torment of abandonment that still gnawed at her insides. When he grew silent, the walls of her protective grotto collapsed and there she was, exposed again to the same old pain.

Radiant, dazzled, she wandered through the voice-cave: the voice of the Singer to the Queen. The voice lifted her and it pitched her downward. It revived and elated her; in turn, the voice grew more sonorous by means of her presence. But when she closed her eyes, even for a single moment, the voice disappeared and instead she saw the line, the hollow, where her ex-husband musician's neck met his shoulder. The contour of it anguished her. She was surprised to see how clearly it appeared to her vision; how the woven threads in his white undershirt followed the line of it, lying so close to her shoulder bone, close to whatever beauty she thought she had, there in the voice-cave, reflected in the sound of the Singer to the Queen's voice when he cleared his throat and began to sing.

The Violin Player had two shoulder bones. He tried to convince her that she had two as well. He said, "It's just your softness that merges them together." But she wasn't persuaded. In fact what she saw in the existence of those two shoulder bones was an exceptional indication of the Violin Player's utter distinctiveness, and therefore also his great fragility. It had made her long more than ever to hold him, to surround and embrace and envelop him, to protect him and to sweep away all the harm that could possibly come to him. Until, that is, the Violin Player became the very harm and the Singer to the Queen—whom she never actually saw—came to be the remedy. But it was the kind of tonic that does not bring a cure. It simply numbs the pain.

"Ghazaala is a strong woman," the Violin Player would tell his friends. A Gazelle!

He must have wished and hoped for her strength, given the many burdens she would lift from his shoulders. The children, all the arrangements of their domestic life, family visits, meetings with the nursery school teachers, facing her family after they got married in the court of law. He encouraged her, at the age of sixteen, to be strong in her love. But when he disappeared from her life, he didn't leave her any prescription for how to go on being strong.

The years she had lived with the Violin Player had folded and collapsed in on themselves as if they had never been. One morning, she woke up to it: here she was, aged twenty-two, alone and divorced and with two children and a BA in business. As more time passed she began to feel and believe that he hadn't ever really been a part of her life. He had passed along her way like the wings of a bird whose feathers barely brushed across her cheek. Lightly, he gave her these two children. Lightly, his beak pecked at the wood that was her life: not to build a nest or even to leave any trace, but merely as a playful bit of fun. Even a joke, she mused one morning. Such a leaden, bad joke, she thought, with a heavy sigh.

When he walked out he didn't leave an article of clothing hanging in the wardrobe or a damp towel lying on the bathroom floor. Not even a fraying toothbrush or a shoe with a rip along the sole. As if these five years had been nothing more than a passing encounter in some hotel one night. The next morning, the traveler put everything in his suitcase and left the hotel room.

She imagined scenes from the past. She could see him sitting across from her after the twins had gone to sleep, playing his violin. He told her that this instrument had been crafted from fine stone-pine wood. As time passed and the wood aged, and the more the violin was played, the music grew in tenderness and sensitivity—like a human being aging well. He had an affectionate nickname for that violin: the Rabaaba's Grandson. Ghazaala had heard the rabaaba on occasion. She wondered whether this stringed folk instrument perhaps had a more deeply sorrowful resonance than a violin could produce. Still, this explanation, like everything the Violin Player told her, she found mesmerizing.

Once she began to comprehend just how humorless the joke had been, she began having endless dreams. In one, the Violin Player would come on a white horse and take her off to a tropical island; she would leave the boys with her family and hold the Violin Player close, night and day. Or in another, the Violin Player appeared suddenly at the door with his beard neglected and his clothes torn, carrying a shattered violin. He knelt down begging for her mercy and forgiveness, and of course she forgave him, and in her tenderness, bathed him and brought him back into the beautiful life they had had. Or in another dream, she opened her eyes and found the Violin Player's head next to hers on the pillow and he was whispering to her that it had all been just a horrible, frightening nightmare and now she would come with him and they would drink tea with milk together. Or a dream about encountering the Violin Player on the street, attacking him with a knife and severing his limbs and tossing them into various rubbish bins. Then—it seemed to happen overnight—all of her hopes ended along with all of her dreams, big and small. All she wanted now was to drop off to sleep with her head on his thighs as he sat following the football match on TV and playing with her hair.

The Violin Player's mother had been a cook at the palace. She wasn't a top-tier employee there, but she did enjoy certain privileges granted to those of her rank. Tirelessly, whenever her subordinates were around to hear her, she repeated that her son's wish was to join the Sultan's Orchestra, but he needed to be granted a scholarship to study music. Her loyalty in service deserved to be rewarded, she told anyone who would listen—and, she would go on, it would not be difficult for her fellow workers to carry this modest request, so well-deserved, to their superiors. It wasn't known in the end whether it was her insistence (and the dear wish of those around her to be rid of her incessant words) that steered her ambitions along that hoped-for path, or whether it was sheer coincidence. In any case, she found listening ears, it seemed. At the age of fourteen her son left home to attend the school of classical music attached to the Sultan's Guard.

The school included accommodations for boarding students; it was akin to a small campus directly facing Qasr Bayt al-Baraka, where the cook, his mother, worked.

The brown-skinned young man discovered that most of his classmates—who varied in age and skill level—had been accepted to the music school following auditions held at their local schools throughout the country. The auditions aimed to establish first whether you had a musical ear. Among his classmates he was very careful to hide the fact that he had been selected based not on an ear for fine tonality but instead on the stubbornness of a mother who believed firmly in the power of connections to make the hopes of her only child come true. Extremely conscious of this distinction, the boy dove into his lessons and worked feverishly. He had chosen violin, defying older classmates who discouraged him from pursuing this difficult stringed instrument and advised him to choose a wind instrument instead, since it would be easier to master.

The more his almost delirious passion for the violin grew, the more he isolated himself from others. The only person he really spoke to was a boy his age who was extremely thin and had brown eyes and remarkably high arched eyebrows, as if he existed in a permanent state of astonishment. The skinny boy told him about his school band. It had performed at all sorts of occasions: the openings of Central Hospital and the wali's new office, a celebration of a new secondary school. They sat in a single row, he said, accordions on their laps, while the girls stood behind them in a second line, singing in chorus and all wearing dresses with high buttoned collars and pink headbands in their hair. Secretly the violinist envied him; he had never been in an event where there were girls present. His school band could barely manage the Sultanic Salute. The thin boy told him, "Once, we went to play somplace in the mountains, for the opening of an experimental farm on the lower slopes. We and our instruments were all packed into a pickup truck, and every time the truck twisted one way or the other on the road through the mountains, we had to protect our instruments with our bodies. It always seemed like there was a danger of something or someone falling out. It was a miracle that the accordion made it there safely, but my head didn't come out of it very well." He laughed as he showed his listener the traces of a scar where he had collided with the side of the pickup truck. But the violin student didn't laugh. He just asked insistently, "The girls? The girls were with you?" The boy laughed again. "No, no, some girls from the mountains joined us after we got there. The wali put on a fantastic feast for us." But now the violinist had lost interest. He went off to his instrument.

Not long after that conversation, this lover of the violin was dispatched to receive a diploma from the Joint Council of Royal Music Schools. He walked through the terminal at Muscat's airport, his face displaying both alert expectation

and wariness. He took his seat at the gate, waiting to get on
the airplane and hugging his bag, into which the cook had
crammed a Qur'an and a photo of the sultan. On the plane
the man seated next to him couldn't have been more different in build and confidence, though he was not much older.
This seat companion curled his lips into a mocking smile as
he asked why the younger person next to him was traveling.
When the violin player—who was not yet a professional violinist—gathered up his courage to ask the young man with
the shaven head the same question, the giant figure just patted
him on the shoulder. These two would become friends over
many years. The Violin Player would learn that this giant
man hailed from the Jidan neighborhood in Matrah, where
many families of Baluchi origin lived, and that he worked as
a bouncer at a bar in London. He spoke English and Arabic
and Baluchi as well as a smattering of other languages.

Much later, after this first trip to London, the Violin
Player would return there many times, obtaining additional
diplomas that guaranteed him promotions. When he wasn't
attached to his violin, he and the giant man wandered around
discovering the secrets of London life that he never would
have imagined if he had been on his own. But what affected
this eager young violinist most, and really fired his ambitions,
was not the Joint Council's diplomas or the amazing little
expeditions with his friend but his striking encounter—as
he was on the threshold of twenty—with the musical legend

Sir Yehudi Menuhin, when he came to Muscat on a visit in celebration of his eightieth birthday.

When the Violin Player met the famous musician, he was dazed by the sudden forces that erupted inside of him, forces he had been unaware of and that he was powerless to explain or even describe. Powers he hadn't known of—but ones he surely couldn't ignore. The twenty-year-old violinist was completely entranced by the old man's halo of authority, the spark of majesty that seemed to emanate from the eighty-year-old violinist, who led the orchestra along with the soloists from the string quartet. The Violin Player could not identify what suddenly inundated his heart as he heard the applause for this public concert. It was as if Menuhin's glory was somehow also a personal victory for him.

Later, he told Ghazaala how his heart had suddenly seemed to split in half like a ripe pomegranate with tens of tiny red seeds bursting out. They all looked alike, but together they formed a prism reflecting the different shapes and colors of life. He shook hands with this great musician who had collected so many prizes. For the first time ever, it occurred to him that he could have bigger dreams—bigger, wider, further. He, too, could travel, and play his music, and enliven big auditoria, and fall in love. The nectar of the pomegranate seeds that had burst open in his heart, so full of hopes, could immerse him and give him new life.

21 May 2011

I'm studying her. She's asleep, exhausted following her chemotherapy dose. Some locks of her long brown hair are still clinging to her head. Her eyelashes are thinner now and her lips have gone pale. Her thin, frail-looking arm lies across the pillow—how light she has become! If I were to try picking her up and hoisting her onto my shoulders, her body would easily submit. But rather than put any kind of weight on me, she prefers to lean on Josephine as she drags her feet into the bathroom.

All of my attempts to be of service to her are met with a firm checkmate. She calls the servant to help her sit up in bed and to slip a single spoonful of broth into her mouth. I scream unconsciously, "Go away, Josephine, I'll feed her!" But she turns her face away at the sight of my outstretched hand coming near to offer her a swallow. My voice rattles in my throat. "Please—please, Mama . . ." And she mutters, so quietly that I can barely hear, "I'm fine, Harir. Why don't you go out and do some shopping? Go to MBK and buy me a wig." She gives me a fake-looking smile.

Josephine is sitting with her head bowed in the kitchen connected to the sitting room. I toss her an angry look as I head for my room. Mama insisted that we rent a suite here at the Marriott—one room for me and one for her, while Josephine sleeps on the sofa bed. Away up here, from the window of my room I can study dozens of skyscrapers. I am thinking that Bangkok is a city of colors. The taxis are painted red pink; the tuktuks are decorated in a huge array of bright hues that remind me of traditional Thai clothing or the rings of flowers at temples—or indeed, of the temples themselves. The women I saw on the way to the hospital today are images that stick in my mind. A woman at a sewing machine supported by a wooden carrying case, her child asleep on the interior wood shelf. Another woman who had tied her child onto her back with what looked like a shawl and was trying to sell her wares to passersby. It is a different scene at night: emaciated girls with heavy makeup leaning against posts while the Arabs and Americans—young men, old men—stop to negotiate prices with them. And then, eventually, they may discover that this girl with her long hair is in fact a young man or that she is a simple country girl and poverty has spit her into the streets of Bangkok. All the same, the licentious parties continue, and the negotiations on the street don't quiet down until dawn comes.

I need Ghazaala. I want to be able to tell her that my mama is getting thinner by the day, her hair is falling out tuft by tuft, and the chemo is consuming her. But Ghazaala only speaks to me during daytime hours. She says that daytime is for work and family and friends, and the night is all hers. But then I discover that the night isn't just hers; it belongs to an Iraqi immigrant living in Sweden, and Ghazaala has a relationship with him over the internet and phone. Yes, that's it—on Facebook, as if she's a teenager.

"But you have two children, Ghazaala," I said to her when I found this out.

Her answer was that a life without love is nothing more than a burial plot a bit bigger than your body.

I tried creeping into my mother's room. In the feeble light I stared at her flattened chest, and the thought came to me that she is returning to her original state. A weightless child with no clearly feminine features. In her room I stared at the heap of balloons that came along with the basket of sweets our Emirati neighbor Aisha brought her. She lives in the suite across the corridor. I was afraid to return to my room— what if she tried to slip out of bed, take hold of the bunch of balloons, and sail out of her open window, smiling that artificial smile of hers that she always believes will reassure me?

I stare down at her tormented sleep. It's as though every breath is scarring her lungs and throat as it tries to escape her body. I'm afraid to push a lock of hair off her forehead because it might just fall out into my hand. I sense my own breathing causing pain in my chest.

That's when I tiptoe back into my room and go back to standing at the little balcony.

What if I were to see my own father down there, bargaining with one of those girls in the street? No, of course not—his status wouldn't allow that. But what if he were going to one of the fancy clubs in this city for a body massage, one body on top of another? What if, at this very moment—I can't help thinking this—he is batting soap bubbles at a whole flock of naked young women? Would he abandon her to the chemo so easily to go and play like that? Why do I get these stupid absurd thoughts in my head? I know that he is currently asleep in the suite on the ground floor and that he will come up tomorrow to say good morning to her, and then, in a quieter voice as he is leaving the room, he will ask me how the night went. He will remind me that his bank cards are at my disposal and that the driver is always there at the hotel's main entrance, day and night, in case we need him. I must do everything she wants, he will say. I know that he will be here again after sunset to wish her good night and say the same words to me that he said in the morning.

The only time he accompanied us to the hospital was on that first visit, when we had to review the tests that confirmed the breast cancer. We were told that a mastectomy followed by chemo were what she needed. We left the hospital—which

Gulf people call the "American" hospital because it is so clean
and the treatments are so good, even though it has no obvious link to America—and as soon as we were in Nana, or the
Street of the Arabs as it is called here, my mother suggested
that we go and have some makbus with lamb before start-
ing the treatment. Because, at that point, she would have to
stick to a strict diet. Her voice sounded as merry as ever, as if
she hadn't heard a word of what the doctors had told us just
a few minutes before. As we walked down the street I had
such conflicting feelings: a mixture of wonder and shock and
total revulsion. The dishdashas and abayas and burqas and
Arab restaurants and sheeshas and Indian shops and night
markets and red-light hotels . . . the international hospitals
and clinics . . . the street vendors, the shouts of people selling fruit and cheap merchandise. The hijab boutiques and
prayer-carpet shops next to rugs displaying explicit erotic
images, women of the night, trans people . . . My mother
chose the Yemeni restaurant that specializes in mandi. The
food was wonderful and the service was terrible. After we
ate, my mother wanted to keep strolling around the nearby
streets, so we went along. Soon my father left us, going back
to his own suite.

Pointing to the heaps of pineapples in front of a seated
street vendor, my mother said, "These are the sweetest pineapples you could ever possibly taste." But I couldn't bear to
think about those pineapple trees that spend six months of

their life to produce one fruit that I could eat in a matter of minutes. Every pineapple plant produces a single fruit at a time. That gives me a peculiar feeling. But I didn't want to share my reactions with my mother. We finished the little tour in silence.

Since that day my father has not come to the hospital with us. Not even once—this hospital that is only a few steps from where we are staying. On the day of the operation he came to my mother's clinic in the evening. All he had to say were a few disconnected words that were meant to console her. Our neighbor Aisha was uneasy; she saw this as a bad sign. She whispered to me that her husband had treated her coldly after she had a breast removed; in the end he divorced her and threw her out of her fancy Abu Dhabi home and put her in a small flat instead. Ever since then it had been her sons who took on the costs of her periodic follow-ups, the examinations at the American hospital. I reassured her that this was not going to happen to my mother.

This was when we began making every meal in the little kitchen in our hotel suite. Josephine cooked with organic ingredients under my supervision and was subjected to very strict rules about keeping everything clean and sterile. Since then, my father has not had a single meal with us. I haven't had the courage to insist that he visit her at mealtime. I guess I haven't wanted him to see my mother swallowing two spoonfuls of broth but only reluctantly, or spilling what is on her plate because the smell disgusts her, or yelling for the household cook—Najib!—who had stayed back in Oman. Four months, we had been living in Thailand. My father flew back to Muscat four times and sent my brother to take his place.

The last time he traveled, to deal with some work issues, I asked him not to send anyone in his place. We were managing all the arrangements fine on our own, with Josephine's and the driver's help, I told him, and the last thing we needed was a child around that we had to mind when he was supposed to take care of us. It was better if Omar concentrated on his studies at the college—where he was floundering—rather than spend his time in the streets of Bangkok checking out all the bars. He didn't say a word, my father, just gave me a rather diplomatic look. He has polished that look over twenty-five years of working for the Foreign Ministry. He traveled to Muscat, but he didn't send Omar to us.

I'm staring from my nighttime balcony down into the street. I see some young men exchanging packets of something, probably some kind of drugs, and suddenly I'm thinking of Salaayim.

One day, soon after the solitary girl on the third floor left the university (for some reason no one knew; she vanished as suddenly as she had seemed to appear), I found Salaayim sitting on the stairs. I sat down beside her. She didn't say anything. She didn't offer any information on the mysterious girl or narrate any stories about the secret marriages of her classmates. For the first time in her recent history Salaayim had no stories to tell. She was completely silent; for once, it seemed, she was absorbed in her own personal story. Yes— now Salaayim had a story, and it was one that she couldn't talk about even if everyone in the residence hall already knew. Her younger brother had been with some other guys. They had everything they needed: meze, injections of tramadol, and the m'allim, whose only function was to watch them and make sure no one took in more than his heart could stand, in which case the m'allim would have to hurriedly open a vein in the boy's hand or leg to let some blood run, reducing possible danger to the heart. That evening, though, the m'allim wasn't paying close attention. He didn't catch on to what was happening to Salaayim's brother until the boy collapsed in cardiac arrest. The m'allim hurriedly opened more than one vein but it was no use. The others had to wrap him in a sheet covered in his own blood. They laid him down at the front door to the family home, rang the bell, and fled. It was Salaayim who opened the door and found her brother, no older than seventeen, dead. Did these men grunging around down there in the streets of Bangkok have sisters like Salaayim, whose hearts they were burning to ashes?

The Singer to the Queen wasn't really a singer. He drew panels for a comics magazine. And she wasn't a queen. She was Ghazaala, or she was Layla. But with him and through him she poured out all the stories she had. His voice was there every night, anxious and eager. "Have the boys gone to sleep yet?" She laughed at this. "Yes, they're asleep." "Tell me a story, my queen." Another laugh. "Aah, child, all the real stories exist in Basra, where you lived your whole childhood."

At that he would protest. "No, no, we'll leave the Basra tales for evenings when we are already in pain. This is an evening for being happy. After all, the latest issue of the magazine has published my images, right? Fabulous distribution! Do you know what my next project is? A graphic novel, something along the lines of the Iranian artist Marjane Satrapi's that I told you about, the one that has become a film! *Persepolis.* In black and white, and some grayer shades in the really intense and dangerous scenes or when things are especially grim. The dark sides of the human soul, and authority . . . you know, Ghazaala, doing this would be the incarnation of what every artist who has had to leave his homeland dreams of doing. But forget that—you tell me something, Ghazaala, tell me about the donkey or the cat that Asiya was raising." That's how the nighttime rituals began. She would talk and talk, as if he were right here, as if his breaths were riffling the back of her neck instead of being somewhere at the end of the world.

"The cat. Shaybub the cat was hungry. My mama Saada told us absolutely not to feed it any of the frozen fish in the fridge. So we waited until she went out to collect neem tree leaves, which she was going to boil down to a broth to treat my brother's fever. We took the scissors from her sewing box. Asiya got hold of the window screen, at the corner where it was already ripping apart from all the dirt and dust and whatever, and twisted a piece off without much trouble. We cut off more with scissors and hid these pieces of screen inside our clothes before running off to the falaj. We went into the water and tried to use the mesh as a net to catch those tiny black fish that you sometimes find in the irrigation canals. We spent the whole day chasing them and we piled up quite a few. Asiya always had a box of matches in her pocket. She lit a fire on the kindling we'd collected, and we roasted the fish for Shaybub. Then we sat down to watch. Shaybub didn't care much about showing his appreciation for this feast we had put together for him with so much effort. He just wolfed it all down, looking around now and then to make certain no other cats were coming anywhere near. I was kind of angry. 'He didn't even thank us,' I said. 'Don't get upset with him,' Asiya said, and she called him over. 'Come on, Shaybub, come and give us a foot massage.' He jumped onto our legs and feet and walked back and forth on them, with all his weight, and we just giggled and giggled."

The Singer to the Queen laughed. "Obviously this cat had his own personality. No wonder Asiya was so attached to him."

She sighed. "The cat died, of burns. And then Asiya went up the mountain and stayed there, in the little cave—the one at the ancient site that people call Kuush Bint al-Nabi because they imagine the shape as the shoe of the Prophet's daughter. We didn't dare touch the corpse. We waited for Asiya to return from the cave and give us our instructions. She came down before nightfall; she didn't have a voice, but she used signs and we followed her orders.

"Before sundown we had washed Shaybub and perfumed his body with the saffron and ambergris we stole from our mothers' manduses, and we wrapped him in Fadiya's green sheet to make a shroud. We put him on a wooden plank and we marched up and down through the quarters and lanes of Sharaat Bat, every one of them, one by one, chanting, 'There is no god but God and Muhammad is the messenger of God.' From their open windows the women cursed us and some of the boys threw stones at us. When it got dark we lifted our homemade bier off our shoulders. We dug a big hole at the base of the mountainside and we prayed. We recited the Fatiha and the Chapter of Deliverance, and then we lowered Shaybub into his final resting place.

"During Shaybub's funeral procession, Asiya was saying something, but it was all under her breath. I was closest to her and I thought I heard the words, but I couldn't tell exactly what she was saying. Her mutterings stuck in my head, though. Sometimes, I have thought that I was finally hearing a word she'd been saying, but I could never grasp a whole sentence. It seemed hugely important, though, this sentence that I had lost."

The Singer to the Queen mumbled a question. "The name of the cave—Kuush Bint al-Nabi?"

His question interrupted the sad heavy pall over the story of the burnt cat. "Yes, there were these marks on the front of the cave that looked like footprints or shoes, and people believed they had been there for centuries. But that couldn't be possible unless they were holy marks, the slippers of the Prophet's daughter herself." At this, they laughed together.

It seemed they would need an entire year to narrate the twenty-four years she had lived and the forty he had lived before these lives could be brought together in their understanding. The Singer to the Queen said, "If I had been in al-Khuwair when you arrived there, when you were fifteen years old, I would have stood at the entrance to Dohat al-Adab School, just to see you, every day, arriving there and going in and coming out again. I would have drawn your portrait, in your school pinafore, a thousand times, and maybe I would have tried to kidnap you and take you on my bicycle and flown with you all the way to Sweden."

She told him that the only meaningful thing about her school in al-Khuwair, even if it was an old and famous school, was the exact moment when she realized that swimming made her well. All of the girls in year ten went with their cheerful, playful teacher on a school trip to Azaiba Beach in Muscat. The beach was practically empty and it was almost nightfall. The girls were completely absorbed in playing ball, not to mention the rare opportunity to eat a lot of fast food. Ghazaala, meanwhile, headed into the sea, easily shedding her school uniform as if she were still eight years old and fleeing with Asiya and Fadiya from Miss Iffat's self-important ranting. Ghazaala had gotten them to go swimming in the pond at the farm without telling the owner, Tahir, Sarira's new husband. Now at Azaiba Beach she could see that she hadn't lost her skill. She plunged into the sea working both arms and legs. It was even better than swimming in freshwater, she felt lighter bobbing along through the waves, and she could keep going without running into any cement walls. She seemed to grow lighter, more transparent—returning to the talents assigned to her by the Zodiac. She was Pisces.

The other girls' yells and the frightened shouts from her teacher didn't reach her. The water filled up the huge emptiness that Asiya's sudden disappearance had left inside her. The white space—the erased space—in her head, her complete lack of memory of the mysterious period between the deaths of Zahwa and Saada and Asiya's departure began to slowly take on more color and substance. Images passed through her mind—real scenes she had long forgotten. It seemed as though these canceled-out memories had found a path through the sea and into her head. For what she had done, she was suspended from school for three days. But she returned to the sea on a hundred days and finally she regained the memory lost to her—the years of blanked-out memory. Swimming saved her. It helped her, or went some way toward helping her, to make her peace with Asiya's departure, when her friend hadn't even said goodbye.

The Singer to the Queen said that if he were walking through al-Waha while wearing a blindfold, still he would know the place, through her stories, house by house. But she corrected him. "It's Sharaat Bat. I don't know why I so dislike the name al-Waha," she said.

"Maybe because of that worker," he suggested. "It was one of the fellows who fixed that signpost in the ground, with the new name on it, and who made the new road, who harassed you."

She laughed. "But Asiya taught him a lesson, throwing stones at him."

If he ever met Asiya, he said, he would tell her he was jealous of her. Ghazaala was taken aback. She had always avoided telling him how she came to hear her sister's voice— and after all these years.

At the time, Ghazaala was still in the Violin Player's home, totally engrossed in the to-and-fro of marriage, home, children, and her studies. She was teaching the twins the alphabet and flipping fish in the frying pan and working on her university research, all at once, it seemed. She was always scurrying after the Violin Player with his food or his clothes. Most hours of day and night, the radio was on.

In the afternoons they broadcast fatwa programs. Most of those who called in were women. She heard one woman say, "Salaam alaykum ya Shaykh," and then go completely quiet. Ghazaala put down the ladle she had in her hand and listened more intently. The shaykh urged the woman to ask her question. The woman's voice came back on, every syllable sharp and firm. "If a person commits a grave sin as a child, does God wait and punish them when they're an adult?" Ghazaala recognized the voice immediately. It was the voice she had grown up with—and grown up through. The timbre of it hadn't changed, nor had that tone of resolution and persistence. Asiya's voice.

Days pass and years go by, but a voice doesn't lose its fundamental tonal color. Radio programs come and go; then the TV channels begin to feature fatwa call-ins that attract larger audiences; instead of one shaykh there are a thousand. Yet on this particular day, Ghazaala happened to hear that one particular voice. A voice she could no longer hear, except across the airwaves. A voice saying only one sentence, a voice that had not altered with the passage of so many years even if the religious channels had all changed. "Peace be upon you, Shaykh. If a person commits a grave sin as a child, does God wait and punish them when they're an adult?"

The voice made no comment on the shaykh's response.

Morning came. Finally. Our neighbor Aisha showed up with a pot of coffee and woke my mother. Mama told us she'd had a dream about her grandmother. She told us a story about playing on the swing at her grandmother's farm and how she had fallen off on purpose despite being surrounded by attentive servants. Aisha laughed at my mother's story, but it made me anxious. I had never heard about her childhood before. How could she tell stories about a stage of life she never really left behind? All her life she has been that same child the servants pushed on the swing, and she annoyed them by deliberately spattering her expensive little frocks with mud. Now the breast that nursed four babies has been sliced off and the belly that swelled with those four pregnancies is flat, even sunken. The memory of pregnancy and nursing has been erased from her body just like that. With an excised breast and a flat tummy, my mother is returning to her origins, in soul and body.

She told Aisha how, one day, her grandmother got her down from the swing, bathed her, and dressed her in a new green frock that she had scented with oud essence and incense. Her grandmother drew heavy kohl lines over my mother's eyes, oiled her face with saffron oil, and handed her over to the women who had come to beat on their tambourines and sing as they processed her to her bridegroom. My father.

He had earned his baccalaureate in Arizona and was hired immediately at the Foreign Ministry. He was living in Muscat, sharing a small apartment with two colleagues. At the end of every workweek he returned to his old room in the family home in Sohar. His very young bride lived there. She occupied herself listening to songs and dancing to the melodies, combing out her long gold-brown hair, and chasing cats and teasing them. She had completed her third year of middle school at Umm Salma School. With her marriage, her education ended. Now her reading was limited to women's magazines, police novels—especially Muhammad Salim's Five Adventurers series—and romance novels, particularly the ones by the prolific Egyptian author Yusuf al-Siba'I.

She had me at age seventeen in that family home in Sohar. But she gave birth to my three siblings in our own home that my father built by the seashore. My father was the sole heir to a rather substantial fortune that his father had amassed in trade, and he spent most of that inheritance on his new house. He designed the seaside house himself. We each had our own room on the upper story, and there was a room for my mother's grandmother. She was very old by then, but she never came to live in that room of hers in our house. She preferred to stay on her farm, cared for by her maids. My mother and father each had their own room with its own door, as well as a small chamber that connected the two rooms, big enough only for a wooden bedstead. Carved into the wood were fantastical sea creatures with lotus petals on their spread wings. With its embroidered silk sheets and carved monsters, the bed was an imposing one, especially since it was high enough to require a small ladder. When we were little we called it "the throne" because it was so high and so richly decorated. Apart from that, nothing else linked my parents' rooms with their separate entrances—neither taste nor furnishings—just as they had nothing in life that brought them together except for children and the throne.

The ground floor was taken up by the various majlises, where guests were received, and then a sitting room, dining room, and kitchen, plus an annex where the cook, gardener, and maid lived. In the large open area was a roofed-over space for parking cars and a highly unusual feature for a seaside house, something people had not seen in such a home: a stable for horses. Was this a house or a farm? they might wonder. How did the many varieties of plants that the gardener tended in the courtyard area grow? For that garden mingled into the sands of the beach, the sharp seaside rocks, and the salt spray off the boulders. How did the horses thrive in that cramped stable? But my father planned all of it, including the connected set-apart rooms that were his and my mother's.

Our Bangkok neighbor Aisha told us many stories about her childhood in Ras al-Khayma, and how she had moved with her husband—who owned a little shop—to Abu Dhabi. There, his wealth grew and so did his social networks. At this point in the story, Aisha started crying, and my mother hugged her. What a peculiar scene! A naïve child with only a few locks of hair on her head putting her skinny arms around a big woman in a massive chestnut-colored wig who was wearing gold rings on her fingers and enough bracelets to cover her lower arms. A fragile child, consoling this woman and wiping away her tears.

After Aisha calmed down and left the room, I asked my mother, "Why didn't you tell her that your grandfather lived his whole life in Abu Dhabi as a pearl trader?"

My mother smiled at me with difficulty and got into bed.

Lying on my own bed I heard a sound like a window being opened. I could see the scene in the next room perfectly: my mother opening the window to her grandmother, the pearl trader's widow, and taking her hand, and the two of them flying away together. Her grandmother would take her to farmyard swings and brightly colored frocks and dolls bought in

Marseille or Paris. Her grandfather would have brought them back with him, a long time before my mother was born, when he traveled there hoping to find pearl markets outside of India. Her grandmother would be whispering into her ear as the two of them circled high above us, the cities on earth growing smaller and smaller beneath them. "I had no business marrying off a playful child like you," she would be saying. "No business weighing down this light body with the burden of a husband and children."

I shouted up at my mother, a tiny dot high in the sky. "Tell her these children give you strength and make you happy, tell her you're proud about having given birth to us. Don't go away with your grandmother, come to us—come back, come back!"

I woke up covered in sweat. I knocked into the furniture as I tried to hurry into the next room. My mother was asleep. Then I tried to phone Ghazaala, but it was no use trying to reach her. I wanted to tell her how tired I was; I wanted her to stop loving the Iraqi immigrant for a little while and come back to me, resume being my friend, without any conditions placed on when I could talk to her. She always jokes with me, saying things like "If a person isn't in love, then what are they going to think about all the time?" Come here, Ghazaala, and I'll tell you. They think about the mother who at any moment now might fly away. They think about food that tastes good and isn't super healthy or sterilized. Oof, am I really as hungry as this?

In the house by the sea, Najib the cook was always in the kitchen. Just as he was always cooking for us—meals that no one came to when they were supposed to come, it was Sunata and then Lakshmi and then Josephine who took charge of feeding us, bathing us, straightening up our rooms, and making sandwiches for school, which we would toss away at the end of the school day because we preferred crowding into the dining hall. Likewise, our neighbors' daughters came up with answers to all the toughest problems in our math homework and drew the maps we were supposed to do for our geography class, in exchange for the crisp brand-new bills our mother showered us with.

My father tried to convince her to finish the education she had abandoned when they married. But when it came to evening classes, homework, and exams, her patience lasted only through one school year. She received a diploma certifying that she had completed the first year of secondary school. But that was it—she said goodbye permanently to studying and went back to her singing and dancing, her cosmetics, her excursions to the shops and the beaches with friends. When my father traveled to finish his master's degree and PhD in London, he tried to convince her to accompany him, bringing the children along, but she insisted on staying at the house on the beach. He had to fetch his mother to live with us so that he could reassure himself that his children were safe and well cared for. She moved into the room that had been meant for my mother's grandmother, and she took everything into her own hands immediately.

I was little at the time. I didn't really understand the arrangements in our unusual house. Especially not my parents' two rooms and the throne room suspended between them like a bridge. I didn't understand why my father's room held a large library while in my mother's room the TV screens grew wider and wider. I didn't understand why my overbearing grandmother—my father's mother—had to live with us, giving us orders and trying to force us to sit down together for the midday meal and then for supper. We used to just grab our meals off the kitchen table whenever we felt like it, shoving aside the beautiful dishes waiting for us. We threw around olives and mint leaves, we tossed out the lettuce leaves that had been folded into the shapes of boats, we squashed the tomatoes that had been carved into petal-like shapes. We gobbled our food down as fast as we could before going back to our cartoons or ball games or teasing the horses.

Whenever one of us bumped into my mother in the kitchen or one of the many corridors, she gave us a big happy smile and a hug, as if we were new toys she had just seen. We would beam back at her and escape again into our freedom. Sometimes her face crumpled when she heard my grandmother ordering us to go to bed or to finish our homework. But she didn't say anything, just went back to her room to continue watching her favorite films on her own private TV.

She didn't show any concern that Omar repeatedly failed to pass into the next year, or that at a very young age Majid was staying out late, or that Faysal had a passion for throwing dead cats into the neighbors' wells.

My father finished his doctorate and was promoted in the Foreign Ministry, where he was named ambassador to several different countries. We only saw him during holidays. He came home loaded down with gifts, but quickly enough he shut himself in his room to bury himself in his books. He didn't concern himself much with his mother's complaints about our refusals to follow her rules. But he did give the strongest attention to one activity that we were not allowed to neglect. Horses and horsemanship.

At age six I started lessons. My father gave me a horse I named Loza. I got very attached to her, and I loved the rides with my father or with my trainer, up there on Loza's back.

She brushed her fingers across the photo of the Singer to the Queen on the computer screen. A completely bald and pale head: Was that out of choice or not? She didn't know. A thick moustache, a light beard covering his chin but stopping before it reached his cheeks. She touched the round metal glasses frames and thought, he's the only person I know who wears glasses with round lenses. He was laughing in the photo. She didn't know whether this was a grin that signaled openness to life or a grimace of cynicism toward life's seriousness.

When she had asked him to send her all the pictures he had of himself, he responded sarcastically. "Are we getting married or what?" He sent her more of his comics drawings instead. They were heavily influenced by French bandes dessinées, and specifically the work of the cartoonist who called himself Moebius. The Singer to the Queen was particularly enthusiastic about Moebius's inking and his use of color; he saw echoes of his own desert images in the desolated steppes that appeared in a variety of psychedelic hues in the French artist's work. Just as art had healed Moebius of the pain of being an abandoned child, it healed the Singer to the Queen of his own childhood wounds and the forced exit from his homeland. She was close to the point of asking him if Moebius was an artist who specialized in science fiction, as she had thought, but for some reason, she held back. Later, when she gave some thought to her hesitation, she realized that it had been her way of trying to avoid hearing any more of his pedantic explanations. Instead of engaging in further discussion, she just told him that she'd enjoyed seeing his drawings in the magazine issue he had sent her, even though she hadn't understood the language of the accompanying story. What she noticed most was that the facial features of his characters were physical reflections of their histories, their personal stories. She also liked the perspective: a bird's-eye view. This remark led him to talk—with great enthusiasm—about perspective, expounding on its influence on his own style. His delight at her interest, and the thoughtful sense of appreciation she clearly had, would have been completely natural and welcome if she hadn't already sussed out that any real criticism would result in him cutting off all discussion out of sheer irritation. On one occasion he had confessed to not sleeping for three entire nights after an article in an obscure journal criticized his work, which he thought completely unfair and unwarranted. If Ghazaala so much as said that one of the panels on a certain page didn't quite appeal to her, immediately she sensed his reaction: bewilderment, even shock, though he might try to conceal it. And then, almost immediately, would come a certain coolness and lack of interest in speaking to her that could go on for several days. This confused her. It made her wonder whether perhaps she was immature in her understanding of these artistic complexities. Anyway, she really loved listening to him, especially when he was talking about his dreams.

The Singer to the Queen's greatest dream was to have the opportunity to study with the Japanese master of anime, the director and screenwriter Miyazaki. The Singer to the Queen dreamed of being one of Miyazaki's apprentices, working night and day in Studio Ghibli, which was producing the most important anime films in the world. He described all of this to Ghazaala, how Miyazaki's films juxtaposed and intertwined complex relationships between nature and technology and conveyed both through his use of fantasy; how, in his films, people find themselves in a world full of violence. Listening to him, her mind was busy conjuring an image of her hand clasped in his and the two of them summoning the spirits of the forest and treating wounded nature.

Maybe it was all of these stories that attracted and held both of them together. So many stories. She only discovered that she had all of these stories inside of her when she met him. Most of her conversations with Harir were about the present, about daily life: the children or her work. But when she talked with the Singer to the Queen it was different. It awakened her mind—as well as the past in her mind, bringing it to life again.

She hadn't felt a love that was so intimate and sweet since being pregnant with the twins. She had sung to them every night and could feel them moving in her belly—astonishingly, they seemed to move according to the rhythms of her singing. Even though she was no more than eighteen, once they were born and were hers unconditionally, she felt like she knew—and indeed, now possessed—every kind of love there could be in the world. It didn't bother her at all to wake up several times in the night to nurse them one by one, or to have to change two nappies at a time. Now, she felt, she had finally been released from the tree where, as a nursing infant wrapped in cloth, she had hung suspended in midair until Saada had caught her in her arms. The fresh new smells of her boys were the real branches—the living green branches— in her life. There was nothing imaginary about them, and she clung to them as fiercely as she could. There weren't many branches like this that a person became so firmly attached to in the world. She had never known attachments exactly like this even if, as a child, she felt the same security and solidity when Asiya hugged her that she felt hugging her boys now. The unconditional love from Saada and Asiya had never come to her again. She understood that this kind of pure, unalloyed affection—and the self-denial it demanded—wasn't something you could find as an adult among other fully grown people. But Saada had died and Asiya had vanished. All that remained to her of Asiya was her voice across TV channels as she sought fatwas on an ancient sin. With her friend Harir, Ghazaala had never broached the subject of Asiya's disappearance. But she did finally mention it in a conversation with the immigrant who was not from here, the Singer to the Queen.

One evening he requested that they switch roles—that she sing to him. It surprised her to discover that she had no songs in her memory. She tried to recollect some old romantic song, or even a fragment of some tune that was popular these days, but she could not summon anything. The only melodies her memory supplied her with were lullabies. Somewhat embarrassed, she asked the Singer to the Queen whether she could sing him some of the lullabies that Saada used to sing to Zahwa. "She sang them while we were jumping rope in the courtyard, and we sang along with her."

He laughed, but it was the kind of laugh that made her feel like someone in this world cared about her and was laughing with her. "Sing away!" he said.

She began to sing, slowly and hesitantly. But then her voice grew stronger over the phone. She was repeating

Saada's melody as the mother grasped the tiny girl by her armpits, tossed her upward, and caught her.

> My luck, beauteous baby, I'd cut my belly
>> open and hold her again
> My luck, beloved baby—grow up and feed
>> your mama then!
> Ya halili, my darling, all beauty is here
> Cherished and held in my eyes and my head
> Ya halili, all beauty, protected from fear

As Ghazaala sang, the words in her mouth spun the coconut sweets that Saada had always made. The words in her mouth were the milk gushing into the pan from Mahbuba's teat at dawn and the sugared buttercream on the paper-thin raqaq bread, all melting onto her tongue. She sensed her voice echoing across the mountain plateaus and the little caves as she gathered herbs, following the trail Saada was making. Singing, she could see the sharp outline of the little babu tree with its globular leaves, which Saada called "the nightingale tree," because nightingales built their nests from its branches. She and Saada were picking its leaves to use as a treatment for eye inflammation in the elderly women who refused to go to the hospital.

When she stopped singing, her face was completely wet. Where did the tears come from? And why had she never been capable of visiting her home village since her family's move to al-Khuwair? She didn't understand. Yes, they had gone back to Sharaat Bat two or three times for the major holidays. But then her uncle destroyed the rooms in the old house because he wanted to turn the house into a cinema, bringing chairs, videotapes, and something resembling a projector to show films on the house's white wall. Her aunt Maliha decided to stay there with him and assist with the project. Once the cinema was up and running, Aunt Maliha would sit on a raised seat immediately behind the main door. How had an ordinary plastic chair gained all this height? Nobody knew. She sat behind a little table with slips of paper cut with care and precision from a school notebook. In large and bad handwriting, each one said: *Cinema Entry Ticket. 500 baizas. Cold drink not included.*

But people didn't acquire one of these tickets merely by paying the sum demanded. Maliha was very keen to scrutinize them first. She relished sitting in this little corner on her raised chair, looking carefully at every person who came in. She had covered over the pockmarks on her face with the Nivea cream that she kept in the little fridge in her room. She put a light layer of Vaseline on her lips before applying lipstick. She dallied as much as she possibly could over allowing the folk of Sharaat Bat to come in to the home turned cinema, in order to make certain that all of them—and she would not countenance any exceptions—had taken note of her presence and appreciated the importance of the work she did. And also, so that the younger ones among them would address her as Ukhti Maliha or—which she appreciated more than being called "sister"—Anisa Maliha. Just like in the films: Miss Maliha! Meeting her scrutiny, the young generally had to face a certain amount of scolding over their dust-filled clothing. Older people submitted to her searching eyes as they adjudicated—without any words said out loud—whether this supplicant's appearance was proper enough to allow them entry into the cinema. When her brother turned off the lights and began projecting the images onto the wall, Maliha would take her seat in a chair with a placard saying RESERVED hanging on it. She had already positioned three cans of Pepsi there, and she drank them one after the other before the first quarter hour of the show had ended. She looked threateningly at anyone who gave a hint of having heard her belch. Or she would be certain to obstruct that person's vision with her constant head movements. The cinema project didn't succeed for very long. After their initial enthusiasm, people returned home to their satellite channels.

Ghazaala's family had stopped visiting the half-demolished house anyway. A frustrated Aunt Maliha moved back to al-Khuwair. Her hopes of succeeding—at something—seemed to have collapsed. She decided to punish the family.

The Singer to the Queen said, very loudly, into the phone, "Have you fallen asleep?" His question startled her into

realizing that here she was, suddenly it seemed, in a different time, where a mere voice could bring her back among the
living. "I really am about to go to sleep," she murmured. She
would have hung up if the Singer to the Queen hadn't surprised her with another question. "Why didn't Saada have
another baby after she lost Zahwa?" Ghazaala answered
immediately as though she had been thinking all her life
about what the response would be. "Probably she didn't want
to allow herself to have another infant. Maybe she wanted
Zahwa to always be the only one and to not be overshadowed
by someone else—and perhaps someone who would look like
her." She wished him good night and went to sleep.

In her sleep, she heard Saada singing her lullabies to
Zahwa.

> Zahwa plays in the water and her father
>   mounts his steed
> Zahwa's with the lady and Papa brings her
>   beads . . .

In the morning her task was to go through the bills before submitting them to the head manager. She tried
to concentrate on the numbers in front of her, but she kept
hearing Saada's voice.

Zahwa's a bride and her mama's bright-eyed
For Zahwa she sings, all silence aside!

She could see Saada's hands tossing Zahwa high and
catching her, tossing and catching. They were not the hands
of her own mother, Fathiya, tossing away a nursing infant and
not catching it. Although her mother had offered to take care
of the twins when, soon after her graduation, Ghazaala had
secured the position of accountant in the highly respected
firm where she now worked, Ghazaala preferred to put them
in a nursery. She justified it to her mother—who still lived in

the building in al-Khuwair with her other children, her husband, and Aunt Maliha—by saying, "It's only a year or two, and then they'll be in school." She had to fight off the sense of shame that came with acknowledging the simple fact that she trusted the hands of strangers caring for her boys more than she did the hands of her mother.

The greenish light of the copier made her eyes swim. Her colleague Afraa was talking nonstop and as soon as Ghazaala put the copier cover down again Afraa leaned on it and kept on talking. The copier was loud and Ghazaala had to shout. "What?"

Afraa raised her voice. "The kiika—it was four layers high." Ghazaala opened the cover and put more pages in to be copied. "Cake?" she asked.

"Yes, the cake!" repeated Afraa cheerfully. "The wedding cake—mine. My wedding."

"Oh yes, I see." Ghazaala nodded. "Great." She put the pages in order and picked up the pile and headed to her desk. Afraa followed her. "You're not going to guess the color?"

Ghazaala sat down behind her desk. "Color of what?" Annoyed, Afraa tossed her head. "The kiika—my wedding cake."

Ghazaala murmured, "Yes, yes . . ." Afraa pulled out a chair, sat down across from Ghazaala and fixed her eyes on her colleague as she asked again gaily, "So—what color do you think, then?"

"Pink?" Ghazaala responded immediately. Afraa sighed and said impatiently, "Habibti—pink is so *yesterday*. Guess again."

The manager was waiting for these pages, waiting for Ghazaala to put them all in order and hand them in. Ghazaala made it obvious that she was ignoring her colleague's question as she bent over closer to her work. Afraa went on talking. "Ooh—*five* layers—and just imagine it, the frosting was the exact shade of natural honey. It was a big surprise to all the guests. Do you know why I chose that color?" Ghazaala smiled at her as she stood, ready to go to the manager's office. But now Afraa was in her way; as Ghazaala squeezed by she winked and asked, "So, do you know why?"

"No, Afraa, I don't know why. Tell me—why honey?"

She laughed and said firmly, "No—no, I won't let you get away with just asking. Think about it."

Ghazaala had many things to think about other than the color of Afraa's wedding cake, but she restrained herself and said sweetly, "The same color as your wedding dress?" Afraa clapped her hands and twirled around. "Br-r-r-a-v-o! A bride in a honey-colored wedding dress? It was such a surprise! Like an explosion! Something really different, something that expressed my different personality. White, white, white—don't brides ever get tired of this blah white that has no flavor, no color to it? But a honey tone, now . . . it's a regal color, you know, very elegant and different, it really does express who I am."

Ghazaala nodded her head. "Indeed . . . Indeed."

A bit later, after her meeting with the manager, Ghazaala went to the little kitchen annex in their department. It was Thursday, end of the workweek, and a late breakfast was laid out for the employees. As usual it was Zanzibari fare—mandazis and kasthuri chana samosas—and tea with milk. She chewed the samosas without any appetite and drank tea, thinking the whole time about Saada's hands and her wet hair at dawn as she baked her bread on the hot metal disk, her tuubj. She didn't recall ever seeing Saada upset or annoyed, except when Zahwa cried—and she cried whenever Asiya made a move to go out and play games with the other girls and boys. Asiya was frequently forced to relinquish being captain of her team because she had to go home and play with her little sister.

The tea almost slipped from Ghazaala's hand when her shoulder was suddenly shaken several times. She jumped to her feet. "What's happening?!" She heard Afraa giggle. "Hahaha, I caught you! You were trying to hide in here so that you wouldn't have to tell me what you think of it." Ghazaala set her cup down on the table. "Think of what?" Afraa slowly shook her head. "Of the honey-color idea, habibti. Sweetie—think about it. My dress, the cake, all the decor. And the plates, and the cutlery—all of it the exact color of honey.

Have you ever heard of Naeema? She does amazing events. Just imagine, even the flowers—real flowers, she was going to do those in honey tones, too, but it would have cost soooo much. Too bad! Oh, I forgot to tell you my tiara had real pearls in it, yes, real ones, a gift from my husband's sister Salma. Now there's a girl with real taste. Do you know how many layers the cake was? Six layers—imagine that! All with honey cream and white flowers. When my husband tasted it, he said it was so good it would make him forget his bride. Such a great sense of humor! Can you imagine what it looked like? Of course, I didn't have two little sugar figurines on top, bride and groom, I really think that's so ancient, really out now . . ."

Ghazaala left the kitchen. Afraa was following her. She sat down at her desk, and Afraa was right there in front of her. She went to the women's bathroom and there was Afraa at the door. She learned that the ring had come from Lebanon—white gold set with three tiny diamonds. And that Naeema, the wedding planner, arranged to bring a band that played local traditional music for a reasonable price. But the girls had gotten bored with "Hayran qalbi hayran" and requested imported songs. Oh well, and this was all easy to describe. But what she had no words for, said Afraa, was the kiika. The honey-colored cake. And so—"Darling, I must bring you the photo album! Tomorrow, I'll have it with me here."

Even though the word *habibti* was planted in every sentence Afraa spoke, there was a sort of half-hidden superiority in her dealings with Ghazaala. "Darling!" meant nothing. At first Ghazaala had not understood this undertone of superiority, but as time went on, she encountered it from her other colleagues as well. These young professional women drew their self-confidence from one thing only: that they were married. It didn't matter to them if the husband was stingy or cruel or unfaithful or a bigot. Only that they had hung on to him—and that Ghazaala had not hung on to her husband. She could see the little gleam in their eyes—as if they had scored some huge success—and she heard in their voices a sort of patronizing sympathy toward her, a woman who was no older than twenty-four and was already raising two children without a father.

She returned home exhausted. She had always hoped to find a job where her workday would end at the same time as the boys' school, but she was caught up in the long workdays at this firm. She admitted to herself that she hadn't been very serious about looking for another position; the rapid promotions and the seductive salary at her company made it difficult to change jobs. Getting home, she always found the twins playing without having changed out of their school uniforms. The food she had left for them in the morning hadn't been touched. The childminder who was supposed to watch them for the three hours after school and before their mother returned from work didn't seem to do anything. She headed for the door the minute Ghazaala came in, calling out as she left the room, "They refused to eat anything." Ghazaala took care of their needs, and then she tried to phone Harir.

"I miss you, Harir. When are you coming back?"

"I don't know yet . . ."

"How is your mother?"

"Well, yesterday we went to Platinum Fashion Mall and she picked up all the silk blouses she saw without looking at the price tags or even the sizes."

"Oh well, Harir, maybe that makes her feel better. Can you still use your father's credit card?"

"Yes."

"Don't upset her, then."

"I don't. What upsets her is the sound of the wheelchair, and that the translators at the hospital speak really poor Arabic, and that she's not allowed hot yam tam soup, and that the king of Thailand is very sick and will die soon."

Ghazaala couldn't find anything to say in response. What was in her mind's eye at this moment were Saada's hands. On one finger she could see the gold ring with the red stone that her husband gave her after Zahwa was born. This wasn't as unconnected as it seemed. She was thinking: What if Saada had scoffed at sadness by shopping, as Harir's mother did? She had a burning desire to talk to the Singer to the Queen about this, but it wasn't late enough in the evening yet. The boys hadn't finished their homework; then there would be the cartoons on TV, followed by dinner and baths. She turned her thoughts to the Singer to the Queen as she moved around the house mechanically completing what had to be done.

His Swedish wife apparently had a habit that she would not relinquish: beckoning imaginary partners to her bed. At first the game had been enticing for both of them; they would agree in advance on the personality they would sleep with: A famous Swedish actress, a French fashion model, a very tall German politician (whose legs would hang over the end of their bed). Their Moroccan neighbor (and in this scenario, he insisted on using very lewd Arabic). His two female Chinese colleagues at the studio (but the fact that there were two of them, and the difficulty of pronouncing their names correctly, demoted them). As time passed, it became impossible to have any fun in bed without these imaginary playmates. Then his wife got fed up with the subjects always being women; this curbed her imagination, she said, and it gave him the larger role. They had to imagine some male partners, she said. Grudgingly he agreed. Barack Obama, George Clooney, David Beckham—they were at the top of the list. Then it was the tennis coach at the sports club in Malmö. And then the tennis coach, and again the tennis coach. Until one day he really did find the tennis coach with her in bed.

There he was, the Singer to the Queen, standing next to

the marital bed. The tennis coach wanted to escape, but the Singer to the Queen blocked his way and made a simple request. To empty his pockets of coins. Then he could leave.

He and his wife didn't bring up the subject again. Days passed just as they had before. One quiet morning he took out the jam jar in which he had put the tennis coach's pocket change. He began shaking it hard, on and on. His wife said she was going to take the little girl to buy ice cream.

A few days later, on an equally quiet evening when the child had gone to sleep, the Singer to the Queen brought out the glass jar again and began shaking it in his wife's face. She tried to leave the room but his big solid body was blocking the door. The noise the coins made echoed and re-echoed through the quiet house. In less than two weeks their marriage was over. His wife left, taking the little girl with her.

O mar phoned. Angry. "How dare you upset my father and get him to keep me from traveling to Bangkok? It's the summer holiday and I want to see my mother
and make sure she is all right."

How did we grow so far apart, Omar and me, when we
were so close as children? I don't know what happened after
that. How did all of those afternoons of naughtiness in the
house at the shore just melt away?

Every afternoon, as dusk was just beginning to gather, the
gardener liked to sit on a mat he placed between the mango
tree and the lemon tree. He would set the tape recorder
down next to him and listen to songs. All we could hear in
these songs that went on and on and on were the moans, the
*aaahhh*s. He was waiting for the cook—his older brother—
to come outside carrying two cups of tea with milk and a little sugar bowl. They would dissolve five or six spoons of sugar

into the tea. Sometimes they had a plate of biscuits sitting between them, or some sweet pancakes. They would get into a long conversation in their language.

Omar and I would be sitting opposite them, pretending we were occupied in some game when we were trying to guess what they were saying. We invented tales, complaints, and grievances, all based on their gestures and body language when they were together. All we could really understand from their talk was their names, repeated over and over: Najib, Karim.

Karim was the gardener. His body had a somewhat crooked, warped look to it just because he was so tall. He combed his hair to the left, and it always gave off the strong aroma of coconut oil. My grandmother would repeat that he was nothing more than a young man with too many grumbles, and that in addition to his whining, he was lazy and he wasn't any good at caring for the plants. He often appeared totally immersed in the songs coming from his little tape recorder; swaying to these tunes, he was so oblivious that the water would overflow and drown the seedlings. That was the moment we were always waiting for. Omar and I would run over to the muddy patch and plunge our feet in, enjoying the gurgling sound they made. Omar, using the mud, would pretend he was hennaing my feet with designs like my grandmother did on her own feet. By the time Karim noticed us—or wanted to notice us—we would have already fled with our muddy shoes, engulfed in some other kind of fun. My father kept Karim on for reasons completely unconnected to the question of Karim's gardening skills. Retaining him was a measure of politeness and respect toward his older brother, Najib.

Najib—or by his fuller name, Muhammad Najib—came to our quarter in the village in the 1980s, before I was born. His arrival was a real occasion. He was among the first Bengalis to come live in the village there, working in service to local people. The first child in his family, he was the vessel of all his family's hopes. He had left home aged sixteen. Soon he was able to remit back his first paycheck—all of it—to his parents. He sent a long letter with it, informing them that he had started working as a cook in a first-class hotel and that he had five associates working under him, doing everything from chopping vegetables to washing dishes.

Despite his young age, or because of it, Najib perfected the art of cooking in what must have been record time. He told my grandmother, in some confusion and apprehension, that his mother had cooked for him all his life. My grandmother brought him into her kitchen and didn't let him leave until he knew how to make proper meat stock, chicken and rice qabuli, cracked wheat and mutton stew, sweet dumplings, and our beloved sweet vermicelli balaliit with fried eggs. He even learned how to turn out perfectly round, perfectly thin and delicate Omani bread—how to spread it evenly across the hot metal tuubj without burning either the bread or his fingers. She taught him how to bake chapatis in a frying pan and how to coat puris with hot oil so that they would puff up at just the right moment. Watching him knead parathas, she shook her head. She explained that these baked delicacies came from his part of the world, from the Indian subcontinent, and she ended her little sermon in formal Arabic. "Here are your good native products, now returned to you." Najib nodded, determined to get it all just right.

When he had her confidence in full, my grandmother let him watch her make the spice marinade for grilled meat: fermented nectar made from salted soaked dates, garlic, turmeric, cumin, and red pepper. She showed him how to spice the carcass before wrapping it in banana leaves, laying the bundle in a palm-leaf basket, and burying the basket in a pit where the coals were already hot. It would be left there for two days. When the grill was brought out and opened up, the entire house breathed the aroma of the spices. Najib went to his friend the photographer's studio. They ran back with the friend's camera to record Najib standing beside the magnificent just-opened palm-leaf bundle. He sent the photo to his family in Bangladesh as evidence of the confidence that this "superior-class hotel" had in Chef Muhammad Najib.

For the first few years of my father's career as a diplomat, Najib traveled abroad with him. He learned the secrets of world cuisines and came back confidently producing

complicated French and Italian dishes—not to mention sushi, which my mother considered the height of his creative
powers. Soon, she got him working at the house by the sea
at Sohar, proudly parading his culinary skills in front of her
friends. No one could compete with Najib when it came to
duck à l'orange, spaghetti with mussels, chocolate soufflé, or
of course, sushi—which her friends were content just to stare
at—that arrestingly bright array of colors on the plate.

Before his youngest brother, Muhammad Karim—the
final and pampered grape in the cluster—had grown up
(enough so that his parents would send him to his brother
in the "superior-class hotel," where he would live with his
brother in the room attached to the seaside house yet equally
detached from it, which allowed some privacy and freedom
of movement) . . . long before that, when Najib had the room
all to himself and I was small, I loved hiding in his room.

I used to creep into it, usually just after dawn broke. I was
a child of the daylight hours, often going to sleep at sunset
and waking up at dawn. I couldn't find anything to do in the
early mornings of our sleeping house, aside from going to the
cook's room. He would have just come out of the bathroom
off his bedroom, having bathed and put on a white undershirt
and striped izar. He would be rubbing his wet hair with a
small towel as he found me crouching on the only chair in his
room. He always gave me a welcoming smile and then hung
his towel on a nail on the wall next to the doorway into the

bathroom. He would come over to the small square mirror that hung next to the chair, pull out a black comb from the plastic shelf beneath the mirror, squeeze a couple of drops of coconut oil onto his hands, and work it into his short hair before he combed it gently, making a center part.

His pressed shirt always hung on a nail next to the wooden wardrobe, which he occasionally allowed me to search and inspect. I never saw anything more than a few folded shirts, aprons, and trousers and some writing paper, envelopes, and postage stamps. There were a few other little, unimportant things—it was all a bit of a disappointment, whenever I looked inside. So I would just go back to watching him as he put on his shirt and reached for the plastic shelf, where there sat a green perfume bottle, its narrow neck encircled by a silver chain. He would sprinkle a few drops of the essence onto his neck.

If my grandmother was there, he would dress in trousers instead of the izar wrapped around his lower body and fixed at the waist; he would tie a chef's apron around his middle and wear a pleated white chef's toque. But if my grandmother was away for a few days on her farm, he would just wear a shirt and his izar, with shiny brown plastic sandals on his feet. Before leaving the room, he would turn to me smiling. My heart would pound as he stuck his hand into his shirt pocket and handed me a globe of pink bubble gum or a strawberry candy in the shape of a heart. Or he would give me Nimr batteries—the ones with the picture of the tiger on them—for my little drumming elephant. But those batteries always gave out so quickly, leaving my elephant standing there, paw raised, unable to beat his drum. It would make me cry. I would go to Najib in the kitchen and moan and complain.

Sometimes he put his shirt on without sticking his hand into his pocket. He would look at me, embarrassed, as he steered me outside and said, "T'morrow, I go shop for buying a batteria, Hareeroo not angry, no." Then he would ask me to stay there with him in the kitchen. From his batch of fresh bread, the first hot disk would be mine. He kept me amused as I waited by giving me a little ball of dough to shape and punch down.

After all these years—after some strands of white had infiltrated Najib's hair, still parted down the middle, and after my father had brought his brother in as gardener and then had brought an assistant cook to help him—Najib still called me Hareeroo. The memory of his simply furnished, neat room with its penetrating, lingering fragrance, a blend of cheap incense and coconut oil, his pressed shirts hanging on a nail in the wall, the pockets full of delights that he showered on my childhood without saying a word, are one of my most beautiful memories of the house at the shore.

I'm your sister Maliha from al-Khuwair," Maliha said to the woman sitting in the chair next to her, waiting for her turn at the diabetes clinic in the Royal Hospital. "But I'm originally from al-Waha."

The young woman nodded politely. Maliha tugged at the embellished edge of her black shawl to make the beads sewn onto it more visible. She raised her voice slightly as she looked around the room. "Al-Waha is a little town, but it's called al-Waha because it really is an oasis." Some of the women looked up from their phones or folded up the slim medical instruction pamphlets that were in their hands. Maliha continued in a slightly louder and more insistent tone of voice. "Al-Waha is a paradise in a desert between the mountains. It's very developed, too. I myself have worked there, in a project to get a cinema going"—she drew the word out and gave it emphasis: the *siyynama*, she said—"and in commercial projects, too, and projects to care for street children." The woman sitting next to her turned to stare at her in amazement. "Is this al-Waha a village? I'm afraid I've never heard of it. I didn't realize there were any *villages* that had cinemas"— she pronounced the word quickly. Sinmas. "And street children. Hmmm, my goodness."

Maliha's lips curled. "Must be a gap in your cultural knowledge, my dear. My brother and I opened the *siyynama* in al-Waha. D'you know the Egyptian film *Kharag wa-lam ya'ud?*"

The woman shook her head. Maliha sighed. "We showed it ten times at least. Fine, but surely you have heard of *Jurassic Park.* The dinosaurs." The woman nodded and seemed ready to return to the pamphlet in her lap. Maliha chuckled. "We must have shown it twenty times. And *Home Alone?* Thirty times. What can I tell you, sister? People flocked to it—never seen anything so popular."

A woman who looked even younger spoke up. She was trying to stuff something into her handbag—the box of incense she had just bought from the woman who was crisscrossing the waiting room with her wares. "But how did you make it work, get the films showing, I mean?" Maliha leaned back into her chair and crossed one leg over the other before replying. She was clearly addressing everyone in the room—all the women who were waiting to be seen by a doctor. "A film machine, that's how you make it work. The machine came to us directly from Amrika, you know. Shipped by boat—it was very heavy. Ooh, if you could've seen it! A huge machine, as big as a donkey, and shiny red, with a gray metal thing it sat on. And yellow letters carved on the side, in English. *Mon Aark*. In English, yes. See, I can read English letters, as long as they aren't all running into each other. What can I tell you? Like it was a little train car. At the bottom there was something like a huge old gramophone, and the same thing right at the top. D'you know about gramophones? My uncle had one of 'em, he listened to Samira Tawfiq's songs. But this machine—the *siyynama* machine? Tuhfa! Tuhfa! What a gem, a real gem! A whole bunch of light coming out of its front end, out of something that looks like the lens of a camera, and then—there it is, the film! That machine would show any film at all. With that thing we saw Arab films, Indian films, American films. Tuhfa!"

The woman gave her a dubious look. But Maliha went on. "And al-Waha, it's full of children who just run around the streets. My brother's daughter and her milk-sister, they were the leaders of those kids out there. Did you see the Egyptian film with the street children? Those devils in al-Waha are just like them. They stole chickpeas and rice from people's houses and went off and cooked them in caves at the base of the mountains."

The woman turned her face away. But Maliha, who didn't acknowledge gestures that didn't suit her, went on. "I used to supervise them. One of my commercial ventures was the fridge I kept in my room. My fridge, it turned into a little shop for the kids. I had everything in there. Lulu soft drinks for fifty baizas. Stoplight ice cream, a hundred baizas. Bu Sahha chocolate, three pieces for two hundred baizas. Chips Oman for a hundred. Strawberry hard candy, fifty. Imagine, my niece—my brother's girl—and her sister and all the other donkeys. Those children tried to feed this stuff to the cow— can you believe it? A huge cow and she would eat anything. She drank Sun Top orange drink from Suhayb's shop."

An older woman across from her laughed. Maliha looked at her accusingly and went on, straining to sound earnest. "I even sold to those kids on credit. Don't have money to-day—you can pay me tomorrow. No problem. 'Cause they were children on the street—they needed someone to go easy on them and take a little care of them."

When my mother finished the course of chemo doses in the American hospital, my father came from Muscat to complete the paperwork and escort us home. We packed and closed the suitcases and sat together in the sitting room of the apartment we had finally rented after a long stay at the Marriott. My father mentioned something about needing a follow-up examination in six months' time. My mother tossed her head to show what she thought of that. "I won't come back for that. Cancer isn't an illness."

My father looked at me with a question in his eyes. I suggested we go out for dinner—we could try the new Turkish restaurant on Si Lom Road. My mother wouldn't go with us. She needed to rest, she said. Getting up from her chair, she said to my father, "Go and find this girl something to amuse her instead of leaving her here. She's always in my hair. Day and night."

Once we were seated at our table my father said, "What's the story with this *isn't an illness* thing?"

"Mother met a Kuwaiti lady in the hospital who convinced her that cancer is just a vitamin B-17 deficiency. And that when she started taking certain preparations, certain fruits—ground dried apricots, for instance—that would take care of it. Problem solved."

My father set down his fork. "That easy, is it?" His voice oozed sarcasm.

I chewed hard and swallowed the food in my mouth. "Yes."

His tone grew almost angry. "That's your mother for you. No opinion of her own. She believes any nonsense she hears."

"Actually," I said, "she did some looking on Google. She found the nonsense there and she also found someone who defended it on scientific grounds."

He yanked his napkin off his lap, making it clear that he was done eating, even though his plate was still heaped with food. "If this is true, then why do governments spend millions of dollars on pharmaceutical medications? So let them grow a lot of apricots instead, it would be a lot easier."

"Maybe it's all to fund the giant pharma firms." I didn't speak with any conviction; I was just trying to counter his sarcasm. But I couldn't hide the edge in my voice, the suggestion of blame. We were both silent for long minutes. To my surprise, he didn't ask for the check but ordered tea instead.

"Don't be angry with me, Harir," he said, his tone gentle now.

"It's not just money my mother needs. It's you beside her, and you understanding her and what she's feeling."

My boldness surprised me. I'd considered myself close to him, on good terms for sure. But the space that my awe of him created always got the better of my longing to speak frankly.

"You don't understand things," he said quietly. "This is the extent of what I can do."

His response made me mad. "Doesn't my mother deserve a little sympathy? Some caring?"

"Don't I deserve that? What about me?" He was almost speaking in a whisper. "Look at your mother. She believes everything she hears, and then she behaves like she doesn't have any mind at all."

I couldn't keep the note of anger from my voice. "That's not the issue. She's sick and she's trying to find some hope."

His words then came out in a rush, as though he had been repressing his voice for years. "Maybe she's in her forties. Maybe she's the mother of four children. But really, she's just a child, a child who can't think anything beyond the easiest ways out of anything. She doesn't care about anything except her own pleasure and avoiding responsibility. Harir, you are more mature than she is."

"You're just saying all this because you're older than her." I couldn't keep the agitation out of my voice.

"The issue isn't the nine years' age difference between us, my dear," he said. "The issue is the light-years of difference between the way I think and she thinks. When it all started, I really did believe that she was just very young to be getting married. But years have passed and she hasn't matured at all. Your mother is as terrified of facing life as ever. She's completely given up even the idea—the thought—of acknowledging that life has to be faced in the first place. She had children because that was what was expected of her. But she hasn't raised her children. She doesn't trouble herself thinking about them or about me or about anything. She scampers after 'freedom' the way little children go after the balloon they find the prettiest and the most tempting. Even the attempts I made to get her to go back to studying were completely useless."

I knew deep inside that he was speaking the truth. But that understanding was silenced beneath my agitated, nervous voice. "Try to get close to her, try to talk to her. Try to involve her in what you care about. Take her out, just the two of you." Even as I was saying these words I felt uncomfortable, like some columnist mouthing sentences in a slickly produced women's magazine where the pat prescriptions for marital happiness blithely ignore the complications of how humans get along.

He was careful to maintain his calm. "What would we talk about? What would we *discuss*? She's not capable of thinking about any issue with any degree of seriousness—let alone talking about problems or issues at home or with the children. Discussion tires her out, it bores her. She really thinks that the best way to deal with any problem is to ignore it. When Majid joined the demonstrators earlier this year at the Globe Roundabout in Sohar, she refused to even acknowledge that there was something happening that might require a decision. She couldn't see that this was a real embarrassment that could harm a man in my position. When there was the epidemic of drug use in Omar's school and I was trying to explain to her that we could work on some strategies to protect him, she just looked at me with those vacant eyes as if I were talking about things that were happening on some other planet, and then she didn't have a word to add. Every attempt at some kind of dialogue, a real exchange of views— it's one-way, it always leads to a dead end. Trying to just have a simple conversation crashes into a wall of miscomprehension. Long ago I gave up trying to build any bridges. I submerge myself in work just to distract myself from my need for an emotional and intellectual bond with a mature woman who could actually meet my needs—my deeper—"

I watched as he stopped abruptly in the middle of a sentence. Had he not felt he couldn't say it in front of me without a sense of shame, I guessed, his sentence would have ended with "my deeper needs—not just physical needs for a feminine body."

I was recalling the way our house was laid out, so expressive of my parents' relationship: the bed suspended between their two rooms, the only connection between them. A relationship that had its only meaning in the existence of that bed. Everything else was beyond the pale of thought or reality.

I understood this, I understood him. But even to sense this understanding made me feel I was betraying my mother. I said, a rattle in my throat, "But she's my mother. She's the mother of your children."

He bowed his head. "Yes, Harir. And that's why I don't want to hurt her, or any of you. Do you think I haven't met, over these years and in all the cities I've spent time in, women whom I felt intellectually in tune with? Women with whom I could discuss ideas, politics, books. And I would see in the woman I was talking with a seasoned, engaged human being who was constantly working to be more and to learn more in life. Of course I could have made a second marriage, but I didn't want to wound your mother or to hurt you or your brothers."

Ghazaala was telling the Singer to the Queen about the new swimming coach, who had received a contract with the Ministry of Sports to work in Muscat. She had left her native land and the many medals she'd won. Coming to Muscat, she had been truly shocked to learn that here it was meaningless to speak about international competitions and female athletes in the same breath. As Ghazaala talked, she sensed the Singer to the Queen losing interest. She caught—even though here she was on the other side of the world from where he sat—the thread of boredom winding along his face. So she stopped talking.

He asked a question but not as if he were paying much attention. "Why are you always going swimming?" She didn't have anything to say. That thread of boredom twirled endlessly in her mind.

She hadn't recounted anything that she figured he was

already likely to know. From a very early age, she had learned to be fearless around water because the falaj had taught her this. She had spent a large chunk of her childhood swimming in Asiya's wake from one irrigation channel to the next, and from an open unsheltered canal into one that was roofed over and dark. Then there was Tahir's farm—Tahir, the new husband of Sarira, who had sworn to her that he would never own a cow. This farm was a paradise for children. When Tahir lay down for his nap, the tight little knot of girls and boys under Asiya's sway would creep in, hardly daring to breathe. They forced themselves to ignore mangoes about to fall off the tree and ripe dates ready for picking because they wanted to avoid any possibility that Tahir—stretched out beneath the mango trees and half drugged by the amounts of rice and yogurt he had consumed at midday—might awaken if they were scurrying around after fruit.

The infiltrators headed straight for the far edge of the farm and the large deep lake that nourished everything growing in the vicinity, its waters pushing through the narrow canals that branched off it. They shed everything but their undergarments and dropped immediately into the water. Some of them were good swimmers and others were not. No one worried much about the masses of bright green moss or the waves of dead insects on the water's surface—or about Hamdan, so expert at trying to drag them by their feet to the lake bottom and holding the heads of the smallest and most fragile among them underwater until they nearly drowned, letting them come up for a gulp or two of breath before pushing them down again. Asiya was preoccupied with tossing variegated pebbles—which she had stuffed into her pockets until they bulged—into the lake. She would challenge Fadiya and Ghazaala to dive in and find the pebbles half buried in the seagrass. How many times had these children come close to perishing here? And how many were saved by sheer miracles—how else could one explain them? The utter lack of adult supervision is what taught them to swim, even as it released them into a state of hilarious merriment. That same absence permitted all of those fake marriage ceremonies on the lake edge at midday, almost every time they were there. Asiya would allow these very young "newlyweds" to kiss each other on the cheek, but she was fierce about not going any further. When Hamdan tried to kiss Fattouma on her mouth, he was punished with expulsion from the lake and indeed from the entire run of the farm. They never knew whether Sarira's new husband, Tahir—"the Pure"—was as pure and innocent as to never suspect anything. Or maybe he just didn't fathom the silly festivities happening at his farm in the searing hot middle of the day and on most days of the week.

But she didn't say any of this to the Singer to the Queen now because he knew it already. She didn't say a word. Boredom. The world is full of words that are not worth the trouble of bothering to articulate. Or maybe they come too late, after the moment when saying them would have carried some meaning or worth.

By now they had already said everything to each other. Stories start to repeat themselves; jokes told twice—or more than twice—fall flat. What Ghazaala said—and she meant it—was "I want to see you—really see you. I'm tired of having just the photos." The Singer to the Queen's response came in a light tone. "But I am planted here along with my seedlings and my canvases. We're all planted here in this house in Malmö." "But your spirit was planted in Basra," she murmured, feeling a bit sad about everything. "Never mind the twenty years in Malmö." He couldn't hear her despair, it seemed; he just went on with his usual light parries. "Well then, you can summon my spirit over to where you are. Call it! After all, Basra is your neighbor."

The Singer to the Queen had lived through his childhood and youth in the city of Basra. He lived his childhood and youth unable to dream of anything beyond escaping the sting of the leather belt that flailed his back more sharply and more often than it ever cinched the flesh of his father, an officer in the Baath army. The officer had two wives and a three-story house. His idle younger brother lived with his wife on the uppermost floor, and every two years or so they flung a new baby down the stairs and onto the next landing, where the army officer's two wives took on the care of this new child alongside caring for their own babies. Each wife had her own room; the boy children all shared another room, and the girls still another one. The ground floor was taken up by the sitting room and kitchen and the room where the officer's mother and her sister lived. And the torture chamber.

It wasn't known who had originally given the room this name. There wasn't even a single whip in there, only benches and a portrait of the president of Iraq, Ahmed Hassan al-Bakr, placed prominently on the wall. All of the army officer's meetings with his sons and daughters took place here. Maybe the room was where he actually lived and slept, perhaps summoning his two wives down there in turn. Or maybe he climbed the stairs to their rooms overhead. The Singer to the Queen didn't remember any of this anymore. There was such a large number of children in that house: full siblings, half siblings, and cousins who lived, more or less, on that floor above them. His childhood was an unending series of fights, and he couldn't distinguish one from the other now because they had seemed to go on and on. They would be cut short only by the voice on the loudspeaker blaring at them on the stairs or wherever they were. Their father's abrupt voice. "Meeting. Now." The mothers had to immediately stanch the bleeding on their sons' foreheads with turmeric and salt. The girls had to straighten their frocks. If anyone was taking a bath they had to come out of the bathroom immediately even if their bodies were covered in soap scum. In a matter of

minutes they would all be lined up and ready to march down
the stairs and into the torture chamber.

When the Singer to the Queen told her about the horrors
he had endured to escape from the army officer's household,
and then from Iraq—the nights of hunger and hiding, of
stealing from place to place and assuming fake identities—
Ghazaala began visualizing these moments as though she
had lived through them herself. They talked about it, but
he wasn't particularly interested in sharing what had happened—in events or details. Or to put it more accurately,
events and details irritated him.

What he liked was singing to Ghazaala and telling her
old stories, many of which were entirely fanciful. He liked it
when the two of them, together, tried to come up with new
endings for the stories they had truly lived. But he wasn't at
all interested in how she lived now: in how she had spent her
day or how her swimming had gone or where she had wandered around with her girlfriend. If she told him something
amusing that one of her boys had said, he just changed the
subject. If she told him she was feeling ill, he calmly left the
scene, withdrawing until she felt better and came back herself, pulled by her attraction to him and once again ready to
laugh and tell stories. She reflected on how insecure she had
felt—being younger than him—and how quick she had been
to attribute any shutting down of their conversation to her
lack of maturity. She felt the wrongness of it.

In the beginning he had passed over any mention of the man she had known before she knew him, the intimate togetherness that had granted her two sons. Then he began asking her—indirectly. He asked her about classical music, the orchestra, musical instruments, and what it was like to play them. He seemed not to realize that Ghazaala knew very little about such things. She had always been fully occupied with the twins and her studies. She hadn't traveled with the Violin Player to any of the cities where he and his chamber group gave concerts. In fact, she had attended only two or three of the national orchestra's concerts, all of them in Muscat. She sat in the audience, her eyes always on her husband and her feelings ambiguous, oddly blurred. It was as though she did not even know the man who had his head bent over his violin, his curly hair almost touching the wood, wearing that black suit, the same cut that every other male concert member wore alongside the splendid red-and-green uniforms of the women who played the contrabass and accordion. Orchestra and audience were framed by the elegant woodwork of the concert hall and the music that pierced one to the soul, as if these instrumentalists were stopping the passage of time with their slim, skilled fingers. The Violin Player looked as though he had always been here in this concert hall, in the very seat where he now sat. It was easy to see that. Ghazaala wished she could take his hand and lead him home. But home seemed remote; it seemed very far away.

The Violin Player had his eyes closed over the music he was playing. It looked to her as though here in this hall he was at home—in his true home, the House of Music, not the House of Ghazaala and the children.

It took her years to understand that his presence in her home had always been chimeric, always in peril of vanishing. He never involved himself in the bits and pieces of daily life. He didn't care whether they moved from a rental apartment to a home they owned with a yard where the boys could play and a garden where they could plant flowers and tomatoes. The Violin Player would never plant anything that might put down serious roots. He would not pound even one nail into an apartment wall where memories might be hung. He would not make a decision on which nursery to choose for the twins or on where the family would go for a holiday. He was the Violin Player, alone in his world and his life—though in unison with his orchestral group. He was the wind, not the roots: the wind that had picked her up and carried her from her family home in al-Khuwair, the wind that took her to the judge's chamber at court to get married without her family's knowledge, the wind that sailed out through the window of the marital apartment after five years of buffeting against its walls.

Her earphones on as she pulled up the covers over her sleeping sons, she listened as the Singer to the Queen told her how he had decided early on to flee his father's house in

Basra. He heard the call through the loudspeaker: "Meeting. Males only." He scurried to the torture chamber. They all did, since for some time now the army officer had not distinguished between his own sons and his nephews. For a moment he felt envious of the girls, but he knew that other arrangements awaited them. In Basra's sweltering summer heat the father made them go out into the courtyard. He waved them into a single line and a moment later, shouted, "Kneel!" So they knelt down on the sharp stones. He had wished he were not wearing shorts but rather trousers. But it was too late now. The army officer shouted again. "Crawl!" They made ten circuits around the courtyard in this position, crawling on their knees and supporting themselves on the palms of their hands.

She wished she could take him away from these painful memories. She made an effort; she told him she had watched one of Miyazaki's films and she agreed with him on the man's genius. He seemed to feel the acclamation in her words and she sensed a change in his tone of voice. But this was the moment in which she discovered that she no longer felt what she had longed to feel. She could no longer count on that feverish sense of longing. That evening in front of her mirror, she asked her reflection: Where did the fever go? Was it still hiding somewhere in her spirit or her body, ready to pounce, to return at some point? Or had it gone cold? She lay down, listening to Katie Melua. "What I don't miss about you . . ."

Harir had just returned from an exhausting stay in Thailand for her mother's treatment. "This is a relationship with no horizons," she said flatly.

It wasn't an absence of horizons, Ghazaala told her, that had demolished the relationship. It was these awful complexes. The Singer to the Queen had never really escaped the belt of his army-officer father or the humiliating interrogations of the torture chamber in the Basra house. Those childhood traumas still had him bound in chains. They framed the entire relationship.

Harir laughed. "If you go into a relationship with a man who has complexes, you will spend your whole life tripping over them and you'll never come anywhere close to undoing any of them."

Sometimes he behaved with a truly childish insistence. When she told him he was acting like a child, he would just get worse. In fact, he seemed proud of flaunting this childish behavior. His attitude vexed her. Did he actually believe that women are attracted to men who act like babies? Did he think that all women yearn to practice their motherhood—their presumed motherhood—with their men? She didn't want to add to his hurt. She didn't tell him outright that most women (or at least all the women she had ever known) prefer mature men. Men who act like adults, like responsible people, not like children who expect to be spoiled.

His craving for praise and his gratitude were his most

visibly childish traits, and the whole thing exasperated her. "I want a real man," she complained to Harir. "Not a forty-year-old little boy who loves to be praised and gets worked up when he isn't."

"Maybe it's the consequence of his father's harshness, the memories," said Harir. "He is still desperate to find the self-confidence that was beaten out of him."

"Let him be desperate for whatever he wants," muttered Ghazaala. "I've got enough to deal with, raising two boys on my own, haven't I? Why am I being so patient with a guy who's not even capable of acknowledging that he was ever wrong about anything? For the most trivial reasons he gets as worked up as a toddler, he has tantrums, and then he expects you to be the one who makes peace."

"A relationship with no horizons," repeated Harir. In fact if there had been any horizons they had already faded, as the jokes and light conversations and fleeting moments of gratification came to replace the blazing words they had exchanged, the loud sighs and the long nights. She buried herself in the hubbub of work at the firm and the never-ending onrush of homework and demands from the school. He buried himself in his drawings and the soirees of Iraqis living in Malmö. Likely, other things pulled them apart, too—enticements, the natural way souls have of following their own sense of allure. But they never talked about any of it. He went on making fancy holiday cards for her that featured his own drawings, and he texted cute little anecdotes. He informed her that he had been able to move to a more important comics magazine, told her when his mother died in Iraq, and recounted the contents of a letter he received from his daughter. She sent him photos of holiday destinations, told him she had finally moved from the rented apartment to a house she had bought with a mortgage after a lot of difficulty, and sent him news about comics in the Arab world that she happened to come across.

10 January 2012

One morning, after we returned from Thailand and my mother began her slow and uncertain recovery, we found her grandmother here in our house on the seashore. She is very old but not so old that she has forgotten how to care for her granddaughter. True, she let go of this role for twenty-five years, but she has taken it up again as fiercely as can be.

Najib makes special meals for her: no salt or sugar or cholesterol. She summons us loudly—me, my mother, and my brothers—because anyone who eats alone is eating with the devil. We eat with her and listen to her tell us the same old stories about her husband, the pearl merchant who had one palace built for him in Abu Dhabi and another in Sohar.

People swore over and over that the man never slept unless a casket of luminous natural pearls was lying in the spacious hollow he had carved out beneath his bed, directly below his head. My mother's grandmother always made light of the tales that had spread about slaves dying from the terrible weight of the legendary casket that they had to carry on their backs from Abu Dhabi to Sohar. "So then—where is this treasure chest now?" she would ask. "No, there weren't any treasures. He lost his trade just like others, and he abandoned the mansion in Abu Dhabi, turned it over to the forces of nature after our son died there along with his wife and left this little girl to us." She would touch my mother's hair, which had begun to grow back, though it was coarser than before.

I give her my arm and we walk out to the area in front of the house, and around the stables, which are empty now. We slow down as we reach the patch where tomatoes, peppers, parsley, and mint are coming up. Chef Najib has been growing them himself ever since his brother the gardener fled. She stops suddenly. "Is there something stuck in my dentures?" She opens her mouth. "No, Gramma," I assure her, "you hardly ate anything anyway." "Take me to the water," she says. I hesitate, even though it won't take us more than a few minutes to walk the path to the beach. She knows exactly what is in my mind, and she turns toward me with her usual cunning. "I'm still young, you know—I haven't gotten to eighty yet. I can walk."

So we go to the beach. We sit on the sand. "Nasir lived on the seashore all his life," she says. "But he steered the diving boats only now and then—maybe more when he was a young fellow. He never let me go out in one. Not once."

"Is it true that he was forty years older than you?" I ask. She laughs. "Forty-two. I was fourteen when he married me. When I had my darling, may he rest in peace, I was fifteen and his father was fifty-seven."

She never mentions her son, my mother's father, without invoking God's blessings: he is always the dearly departed one, may he rest in peace. She always calls her husband simply by his name, Nasir, never using that term of respect for the dead. The two of them died in quick succession, within two years of each other, but only her son is "the dearly departed one." Al-Marhum.

She sits there on the sand, her back straight, and it's obvious how thin she is. I want to ask her how she felt when she was married to the old man who had been widowed twice before he met her and had seen five sons die. But I know that she will just give me her sly little smile and won't say a word.

I nudge her shawl around her shoulders. She murmurs, "There weren't any caskets of pearls hidden away. He lost it all, like the others did." She gets to her feet, leaning on me again. I brush the sand off her clothes and we return to the house.

Nasir was born at the end of the nineteenth century. His father named him Sultan. Throughout his boyhood he struggled with fevers and other illnesses. Finally he said to his father, "I am not Sultan. It's not the right name for me." His father didn't know what to make of it. But his son insisted and he refused to answer when anyone called him Sultan. In despair the father asked, "So what is your name?" "Nasir," he said. "My name is Nasir." So it was. And then, having named himself "the One who Triumphs," he recovered from all his illnesses.

He had hardly crossed the threshold into young adulthood when he left Sohar to join his uncle, a pearl trader in Abu Dhabi. With sharp natural intelligence and a blazingly smart mind, it wasn't long before he had learned the basics of the trade. In fact, he soon became self-sufficient. He did what was called "lone diving." That is, he avoided going into debt to a dhow's nukhadha as so many other divers found themselves forever bound to their ship captain. He would secure a place on the dhow, but instead of paying for his berth he gave the captain a percentage of the profits. In a few years' time he was able to buy his own dhow; now, he no longer went out on his own. While Japan was developing its cultivated pearl industry, this strapping young diver was taking to heart the words of Muhammad Bin Thani, the ruler of Qatar: "From those of us with the highest status to the lowliest slave among us—we all have one master: the pearl." Throughout his long life Nasir made obeisance to this shining master. He made his trade independent of his uncle, and he eventually owned no fewer than fifty of the four hundred dhows that clustered in the harbor and crowded the shore of Abu Dhabi Town.

In his early thirties, when it was more than clear that the ship of his life had anchored itself to the throne of the pearl, the global economic crisis suddenly loomed. It shook the throne that had seemed so sturdy. He continued to finance expeditions during pearl season, and he loaned money to the nukhadhas who captained the diving dhows and were responsible for feeding and clothing the crew, the divers, and the men who were expert at pulling them up from the depths, calculating exactly how long they could remain below the surface. Meanwhile, the voices of divers who had sent petitions complaining of poor labor conditions to the British resident in Bushire did not quiet down. They were not paid enough to live, and these new pearls cultivated in Japan cost one-tenth the price natural pearls commanded. But none of this stopped Nasir. He could not imagine the magic of it coming to an end—those moments when he would receive the most beautiful, largest pearls from the dhow captains and would sit at one of the tables in the many structures erected on the seaside to provide a secure and quiet place where he and the other pearl traders could negotiate prices in their wordless way. The hand of the seller and the hand of the buyer would be thrust under a red velvet tablecloth; they came to an understanding through signs concealed from the eyes of all the other merchants as they, too, pursued their hoped-for bargains. The magic was all here, hidden beneath the velvet. It didn't reside in the magnificent home he had built on the water, or in the pearls that adorned his two wives' throats, or in singing or listening to the songs that divers had long sung on the hot evenings. The magic was here in the game of fingers that held promises of fortunes beneath the red table cover.

Nasir was not a dreamy person, though, nor a man ruled by illusions. When the fleets of pearling dhows grew fewer and fewer, and the workers in the five hundred jobs associated with this enterprise began racing each other to emigrate else-where in search of income, he swallowed the loss by widening his trade to include gold, silk, and spices. His vessels still went out but now with increasing resistance from the divers, who were accustomed to making 150 dives or more in a single day. And the sayyibs—those men who pulled the divers up from the deeps—all the while in constant terror of getting it wrong and betraying the trust placed in them. What if their attention strayed or they weren't quite quick enough hauling up the ropes, lest their mates the divers drown or be swallowed by sharks or impaled by jittery swordfish? The divers were heavily weighted by the debts they carried, owed to the nukhad-has. Some had inherited these debts from their fathers, whose own fathers might have bequeathed this burden to them. Hence the flight of indebted seamen to the oil companies that were suddenly all over the Gulf region. But the decisive blow for Nasir was not the recalcitrance of divers in the late 1940s coupled with the prohibition of pearl imports imposed by the new Government of India. It was his personal catastrophe. His two wives died one after the other, as did all of their children, decimating his dream that they would inherit his trade and the large villa he had been renovating and expanding.

Nasir did not give in to his grief. He told his friends that he would live long enough to father a son who would elude the clutches of death and would grow old enough to strap his father's dagger to his own waist. In his fifties, Nasir returned to Sohar to pick out a new wife: this young girl who was now nearly eighty years old and still wore a double strand of natural pearls down her chest. This young girl who, from the very beginning, had concealed in her thin form a determination that would never go soft, a force that kept her able into old age, after years of enduring the sorrow of her only child's death along with his wife, electrocuted in their wing of the villa on the Abu Dhabi coast, leaving to her the fragile, still-nursing baby girl who became my mother.

Her husband, in his seventies by then, could not endure it. He abandoned his villa in Abu Dhabi, witness to so many glories and so many losses. With his mourned son's dagger on his belt, with his granddaughter and his wife who became, in her midthirties, a grandmother and a bereaved mother both, he returned to Sohar, where he died and was buried.

A nd then the Violin Player came back.
He walked into the new house—Ghazaala's
house—and he sat down on the sofa.

The sitting room had a curved wall with bay windows
nearly to the ceiling. It was Ghazaala's favorite room. She was
impatient for the seedlings in the garden to grow so that, sitting comfortably on her sofa, she could gaze at them through
the windows. The sofa was a restrained white with cushions
in bright tones. It was here that the Violin Player sat down,
apparently exhausted.

Ghazaala was still the mother of his children, he said.
Ghazaala was his friend. And he was ready to do as she
wanted. He would visit the twins. He would pay for private
school. He would take them to the swings in the park, to bar-
becues. He would go with them to the Trade Center, where
they could play electronic games. In the autumn he would

take them to the southern town of Salala, and in the summer to the beach.

He had a few white hairs now, around his temples. Ghazaala remembered seeing him once on the street, not long after their divorce, and noticing that his shoulders looked slumped or half collapsed, as though deep cuts had been made in his neck. He was walking alongside his friend the giant of Matrah, she had noticed, and he looked a bit shrunken. Images from the final days of their marriage passed through her head—the days she had thought would last forever. But those days had broken into fragments, and then the fragments had vanished when the Violin Player left the house for good. The giant had been waiting for him at the wheel of his car. In her mind flashed the figure of the giant with the Violin Player walking in his shadow: the enormous shadow submerging the gaunt violin player. That shadow directed his movements and at the same time swallowed him up.

Now, leaning back against her sofa, he couldn't seem to stop talking. And he said he wanted to go on talking with her—as a friend. He wanted to drop by the house and have a cup of coffee with her on a regular basis—as a friend. Maybe he would have some complaints to make about his colleagues or his new wife—to her, as a friend.

Years had passed, he said, and they were older now; they were mature people now. He had left the orchestra, he told her, and he was in private business. Plant nurseries. He didn't want to stay in Morocco any longer. His wife, who was Moroccan, had caused him problems. He needed Ghazaala, he said. As a friend. He needed her.

She had thought that if the Violin Player ever returned she would consume him with her desires. It would be as simple as that. How she had burned—consumed herself—with the desire to be his beloved once again! The craving to see the heart that had frozen against her to now melt and return to her, to open like a magic box and beckon her in. How much, how often, she had been tormented by her longing to go inside that magical space; by her desire that the Violin Player's heart would close around her and not leave her outside in the cold beyond its windows. But the only heart whose windows she wished would break for her sake instead had locked those windows as tightly as could be.

She didn't want the cold state of "being friends," or the iciness of "fondness" or "sympathy," the cool distance of "spending time together" or "niceness." She wanted the fire of love. Nothing less than a full flame.

But she didn't say a word. She left him to ramble on in the sitting room of her house, which she had purchased on installment and furnished on installment; where she had planted a garden of trees that were putting down roots. She went into her bedroom, shut the door, and went to sleep.

She had a dream. The main falaj canal in Sharaat Bat was surging in the opposite direction to its usual flow. It began at the orchards on the edge of the village and ran to the foot of the mountain. It ran up the mountain, passing the cave of Kuush Bint al-Nabi, until it branched and reached the peaks that encircled Sharaat Bat. The waters were abundant and the canal's reversed direction didn't seem to surprise anyone. When she woke up, it wasn't the coldness of the friendship offered in the sitting room that she sensed hovering. It was Asiya, whispering. She had been hearing that whisper for years, and she had tried to make it out; she knew where it was coming from. But now she heard these words as though they were being said for the first time. Or as though the falaj in the dream, reversing direction, had somehow given these words clarity. As if the quiet rustle of Asiya's thick hair was still against her neck as she whispered, during Shaybub the cat's funeral, "How beautiful it would be if this were the funeral of a human being."

My jealous husband asks me if I was ever in love before him. He won't believe that I got to the age of twenty-five, and lived abroad for an entire year to get my master's degree, without getting to know anyone. I guess there were some momentary attractions and half-hidden flirtations, but I am being absolutely truthful when I tell him that I was never in love before him. To be a little more precise, I should probably say that I was never in love, since I don't know whether the affection and understanding we share can really be called love. He is the brother of the director of the Arabic section at the international school where I work in Muscat. The director kept saying to me, "Harir, mashAllah, you are soooo pretty, you are really gorgeous." Then she grilled me about my family, my friends, and my tribal affiliation. When she felt reassured on that score, she invited her brother—a PhD student writing his dissertation on the

Omani irrigation canal system—to the school to see me. As if it were all by chance. When he was sure of his wishes, he introduced the idea of getting engaged. We met twice with her, and then we met once with my brothers present. My family wanted to know all about his family, his friends, and his tribe. Then they agreed. We lost ourselves in extended phone conversations, and within a year I found I was a wife and a mother.

I whisper back to him. "No, no. I never loved anybody other than you."

Looking at his face I close my eyes. What pierces me is the gaze of the girl who covers her mirror with brown bookbinding paper. I can see the tiny picture at the center of that covered mirror, in that room in the women's residential block. The little girl with hair pulled back and a short ponytail, her eyes sparkling and her cheeks full. Ya ilahi! How much that girl seems to have in common with the possessor of the mirror—it could be her as a little girl! But I know now that it isn't.

The image of her long abaya flashes through my mind. I see her hands, without any kind of adornment, and I pick up the traces of her earthy scent, like old fruit. The girl who barely got to know me and whose memory torments me without my knowing exactly why. But—why did she just barely get to know me? Where did that long evening vanish to—the evening when we walked together around the university buildings with my hand nearly lost in her much larger hand? Why did I think, after that evening, that I had entered into the grace of her acceptance? That she would erase that expression from her face, the look in her eyes that seemed not to see me; that she would look at me the way I looked at her? I stood many times beneath her newspaper-covered window, staring upward to try and decipher when the light would go on or off. I counted the number of floor tiles in the halls and on the stairs between my room and hers, tile by tile, my room to her room, but I wasn't invited to go in. And then she vanished.

Have as many years as this really and truly passed since I discovered she had vanished? Where is time anyway? How can it pass us by like this—like a river that flows on and on— and then how can it simply stop as if assaulted by a winter freeze? Where do the hours and the days flow and end up, or the weeks and the months? Where do they hide themselves, how do they slip into the shadows, leaving the heart raw and deluded as if time were nothing more than a game of illusions, a sparkle that dies when a stream of water is poured over it?

When I learned she had gone I didn't believe she could just disappear like that, vanishing so suddenly from the corridors and the courtyard and that wing of the building and the third floor. Could disappear as though she had never existed. I hurried to her room. Empty. The cleaner had just left and the door was open. There were no traces of her inside except her lingering scent. I wished the pores of my skin could inhale her smell and trap her inside and let me cry. The child's photo was no longer there. I tore the brown bookbinding paper off the mirror, strip by strip, until I could see the entire glass. Scratched into it I saw words. ASIYA SINNER ASIYA SINNER ASIYA SINNER.

So had this span of time been nothing but a deceitful trick? There was no *time*, not really. For the heart had stopped beating in that moment; it had bared its feet on the threshold and stopped. It had not moved. Time had not moved. Water was poured over its flame to extinguish it. But—what water?

If only a person could choose the water they will pour over time to quench it. If only a person could choose when to pour—and then stand firm. And when to leave it be—and then let it pass quietly by and revert to a course fixed by eternity. If only one could choose. This face is theirs to show, and that one is not; this step is theirs to take, and that one is not. If that were so, if one could choose, then what fortune would bitterness have with the heart? We would pour water over our bitterness and put out its flame.

Time has slithered along like a viper and settled inside the cracks of the mirror and the fissures of the days. And then, if the mirror remained as it was, still and silent, the cracks would open and widen, and time would slip through. But the viper grew into a ghoul and the ghoul turned to face me.

Who are you?

I am Time.

It's been said that you heal wounds—that you don't in-flame them and make them worse.

Well, that is only when I am running on and when my footsteps can melt away into the past. But here I am, lying in wait for you and ready to strike.

Why are you a ghoul?

But I was never anything less than that.

How can I kill you, when you are everlasting and I am a fleeting creature? How can I tame you, when you are the one in charge and I have no power to wield? You are Time, you are the ghoul, and I am a mere human. The game you play is so strange, so alien; I am completely incapable of under-standing it.

What would have happened if the words had not been said? If Asiya had not breathed the secret? What would have happened if those steps had not been taken? If I had not fol-lowed her down every corridor? What would have happened if the route had remained familiar and known, indetermi-nate and definite, all at once—and if it did not call out that one must follow it?

What would have happened if I had stopped and stood still exactly where the firm pressure of the boundary, like a determined hand pressing against my chest, was trying to make me stop?

What if I had told myself *no*, when *no* was the truth, and had remained silent. What if I had refrained from saying *yes*, when *yes* became the reality I saw before me?

Where has my resolve gone? Where is the knife, the dagger, determination's weapon that would keep me poised? I can see only my own brokenness on its threshold.

It bled me, without even pulling out its dagger. I was shattered with every twist of that knife-edge of disregard. The reproaches in my mouth scarred me. Silence pained me as much as words wounded me. I tried to confront all the harm the beloved had done. Did you really mean to hurt so much! The beloved wasn't intending to inflict such injury by sharpening that knife, surely? But the pain mocked me. The pain taught me that intentions have no meaning when deeds speak up. Knowledge is a harsh and merciless light. I wish the pain had not taught me anything. I wish the pain had not forced me to sit down and listen to its lesson.

The Year of the Elephant

In the Year of the Elephant, the elephant entered the ceramics museum and knocked over a gazelle. His dumb unknowing trunk smashed everything to bits.

The first time they met, at the fish restaurant, he asked her, "What do you dream about?"

"Becoming an ant," she said.

He laughed. What was there to laugh about? If she were an ant she would go wherever she wanted. She could have crawled up onto the elephant's back and planted her tiny body there. She would still be clinging to the elephant's back so as not to fall off and be crushed by his huge stumpy legs. But she wasn't an ant. It was only a dream. She rolled off the elephant's back and he stomped on her and she was no more.

He had been transferred to her division in the firm a few months earlier. He settled into one of the tiny offices that were separated by glass-and-wood partitions. Every whisper could be heard through those flimsy walls. If she needed to call the twins—because she had to tell them something that couldn't wait—she had to go into the kitchen so that none of the eight employees (some of them women, some of them men) would hear the instructions about how to warm up their pizza for lunch, or where their socks and running shoes were, or that she would ban their iPad use if they didn't stop quarrelling with each other immediately.

Months passed before she realized that his existence on this planet had changed her life, however slight that shift might have been and even though he might as well have been dwelling somewhere remote when it came to the daily routines of her life. Once, she asked him, "Why aren't you wearing a dishdasha like all the other men who work here?" He laughed. "We're in a semiprivate company, we're not under any obligation to wear national dress. Why aren't you wearing an abaya like all the other women who work here?"

She almost said, "Because the Violin Player doesn't like black." But then she reminded herself that the Violin Player had left her life years ago. Had the Violin Player smacked his instrument against her spirit, leaving a permanent imprint that would mark any choice she might ever try to make? Or was he simply an old tune that was finally, gradually, fading away as though it had never hovered around her ears? She smiled at her coworker and said, "Because I don't like black."

He had to pass by her desk first thing in the morning. She

would get a whiff of the cologne he wore, Boss. At the end of the afternoon and after a tough day of work, as he walked by again, she would smell something else, an earthier body smell that reminded her of her early adolescence. Back when Asiya used to shove Ghazaala's head into her armpit in order to prove without a doubt, and with a lot of pride, that hair had started to grow there before there was any sign of it on Ghazaala's underarms.

He would pop his head over the partition and then come in, saying he wanted to confirm some bit of business or to have a quick chat. The sweetness of it shook her, but she didn't understand from where this sensation was welling up. His voice was a bit rough, his hand a bit coarse-looking, and there was something a little loud about his presence. Yet she found herself almost dizzy from an onrush of something delectable.

He gave her quick little glances as he spoke, almost covert glances, while she gazed at him steadily. She studied the buttons on his shirt, musing about how the seamstress at the factory must have picked up each one and sewed them onto this shirt, button by button, so that now its edges met smoothly over his chest and so that the seamstress could make enough money to feed her children dinner. She thought about how the merchant selling the shirt had hung it in his lit-up shop until this man took hold of it and laid it on the counter to pay. How it rested in the laundry hamper until the washing machine put it through endless wash and rinse cycles. How the makwaji at the shop pressed it and delivered it to his home. How he put his arms through the sleeves and buttoned all the buttons and took a step, and then more steps, until he put his head over the partition and came in and sat down facing her and began to speak, while she was thinking about the onerous voyage this shirt had made all the way to his body.

She stared at his forearms. The skin at his elbows was peeling. An image of skin moisturizer came into her mind; the jar was either sitting in her cabinet at home or she had seen it in the skin care section at the supermarket, or maybe on her aunt's cosmetics table. She was a bit startled seeing how the hair on his arms grew as far as the backs of his hands. What she was really seeing, she thought, was how a child's soft skin gradually becomes clothed in hair, announcing that the child has become a man. And every hair on him was still growing, silently—on his arms, chest, face; stopping only at those fingers: the smooth fingertips that might have brushed lightly across her cheek. Those fingers now gripping the chair; she could feel the leather compressed beneath his fingers. When he left her office, she would rest her own hands just there, on the leather.

She studied his neck, emerging from his shirt collar without any particularly distinguishing feature. Inside the collar, she wondered, far inside, what would the inside of his throat look like? When he caught a cold, she imagined how it would change, swelling up and reddening. And he would say—if she were to suggest that he have some honey with lemon—that it would make him throw up; she felt a desire to witness it. He was sitting there facing her as he spoke, so she couldn't see the back of his neck. But she already knew there was an ancient dent there, a small circle of rough skin that might have been left by a burn long ago or by a collision with a sharp object. She asked him about it once, but he said he didn't remember. It pleased her that she had found a distinct and unique trace of his past on the back of this very ordinary neck. Once, she had the sensation that no more than a wafting thread of air separated her fingertip from the ancient burn mark.

She studied his jaw. It wasn't wide but it wasn't unusually narrow, either. Mostly the jawline looked smooth and soft, occasionally rougher where a few stray hairs had sprouted. She began wondering what kind of shaver he used. It must still be damp, sitting in the bathroom in his home, possibly tossed down a bit carelessly next to the sink or maybe put carefully back in its usual place. She could see drops of water like tears welling up on his shaving brush. At the mere image, salty tears began to form in her throat.

She stared at his thick black moustache and his mouth. Thin lips pressed together; nothing to suggest the faintest hint of sensuality. But there seemed a hint of violence in their firm closure—a very thin feeble imprint between and inside those lips. A concealed hint, yet she could see it clearly. And she knew that if she could pass her tongue along that closed-up, unyielding line, she would just die of its tangled cruelty.

She gazed at the slight arc in his nose, the few hairs on it visible when light bounced off it. She imagined the moments when each hair broke through the skin and grew at its own pace on this remote promontory, the arced tip of his nose.

His eyes: no matter how long she gazed at them she couldn't fathom anything. All she could see in those eyes was her inability to understand. She tried to go into their depths. She wondered about those eyes, closed, in the instant when he came into the world, and then how they would have opened in the joyous gaze of his mother, how they would have changed color through the years of his childhood and youth, how they would cry. Cry? No. She had never seen his eyes tear up, even though he had told her that Muhammad Abdo's song "All Places" did make him weepy.

She stared at his eyebrows, the tiny hairs going every which way. They looked Chinese, she thought suddenly. His forehead: creasing up and then relaxing, the expression on his face changing as they talked. His mind, she thought, was hidden away back there, somewhere behind this brow and under all of this black hair. She tried to imagine his brain, the twists and turns, thousands of thoughts running through all of those channels, thoughts she didn't know, and thousands of sensations and feelings she wouldn't understand. He was thinking but she couldn't see into his mind.

She studied his hair, sensed the sticky hair gel where his hairline met his forehead. Thought about the hair flattened behind his small ear and how the thickness of it decreased as it reached his neck. There would be little thoughts in the back of his head and tiny drops of Boss on the skin of his neck. The bottle would be empty and he would drive his little black Citroën to the Trade Center to buy a new bottle. As he purchased it he would be wearing these same gray trousers and the wide leather belt and trainers. Were she to hear the sound of these particular footsteps in the distance, she would recognize them.

As he spoke she stared at his teeth and tongue, and at the same time, she was thinking about the words that were coming out of his mouth. These words that flew around in the circulating air of the firm where they worked; these words that sailed through the air and came to rest however and wherever they wished. As all of these words were moving through the air here in this office, she went on gazing at him steadily and gazing at the words as they settled and spread and grew denser—in the air, on the walls and chairs and on her clothes. All the while, she was looking steadily at him.

They lived in the same part of town, she discovered. This was a frightening realization. Between her and the Singer to the Queen there had been a distance of six thousand kilometers. He had teased her by saying that he would need only 2,200 hours to reach her, coming on foot. But in the moment when she felt she needed him, she had only to pick up her phone. That was all: reach for the phone and there she was on the garden path to the Singer to the Queen.

But the Elephant—this was a different story. He lived within a five-kilometer radius of where she lived, yet he was more distant than the remotest star in the sky. She would climb into her car and drive off through the few streets she needed to traverse, from an intersection to a traffic circle, from a curve to a straight stretch of road, and every single black Citroën she encountered nearly made her lose her equanimity. She would try to steer close enough to see the number plate and model. Maybe it was that one, parked alongside the shop over there; perhaps he had forgotten to buy milk for his little daughter. Coming closer, she could see how shiny the car was. No, his car was not as new as this one. She would resume her drive home but she never seemed to arrive. "When will I get there?" she asked herself, and she was still asking that question as she snuggled beneath the sheets between the sleeping twins.

Finally, it dawned on her that when she began to shiver toward the end of the day it was not because the air-conditioning in the office was set so high. It was because of his scent. She began following his scent without being fully aware of what she was doing: through the corridors lined with partitioned-off cubicles or into the little corner kitchen annexed to their division, where the teakettle sat. All the desires she had in the world seemed to have emptied themselves out, except the longing to push her head into the space under his arm as Asiya had made her do, leaving her to take in the scent until the world came to an end and life could sink out of sight like the sunset.

Once, she did catch sight of his car. It really was a black Citroën, and there he was in the driver's seat. She followed him, around every curve and down every lane, around every traffic circle and through every intersection. Would he come to a stop in front of his own house? No, he was going past it, she was behind him, she could see a bit of his hair through the window, even though the glass wasn't very clean. She could see the edge of his hand as he put his arm out to flick the ashes off his cigarette. She couldn't feel her own fingers around the steering wheel; she had no sense of her own body sitting there at all. "What am I doing?" she asked herself. "What am I doing?" But she didn't veer a hair from the straight path made by the black Citroën's tires. She caught flashes of the license plate whose number she knew, but it felt as though she were gazing at some miraculous, completely unexpected sight. Her eyes were fixed on the license plate as if she were simply following those numbers, nothing else, nothing more. She no longer saw his hair or his arm or the street or the traffic circles. Her entire focus was on those numbers, as if the numbers themselves were leading her forward in her blindness to everything else.

Finally the car stopped at a petrol station. She stopped her car. He waved at her and so she parked and got out. He opened the passenger-side door and she climbed in to sit next to him. She was trembling. She didn't turn to look at him. He started the car and as they drove, she imagined she was hearing songs of some sort coming from the radio and she heard him ask her how she was. But the one thing she was truly aware of was that she was trembling. His hand closing over the back of her hand only made her tremble harder. He stopped the car in front of a small restaurant and she got out. He chose a secluded corner and she sat down. Suddenly she felt terror. What if he abruptly said something like "Why are you following me?" But he didn't say it. He ordered two plates of grilled fish and two lemonades. He didn't ask her whether she liked grilled fish or lemonade. When she stopped trembling he was looking at her, his eyes radiant. Now she could breathe.

She wasn't hungry but it embarrassed her not to eat. When the plates were finally removed from the table, he pushed his chair back and lit a cigarette. He told her that he had been hoping for some time that they would go out together. He constantly imagined that he would invite her to have some of his favorite fish dishes and that she would sit as close to him as she was now. This was pure joy, he said, having her near and being able to take her hand.

He ordered tea. She told him about the mountains en-
circling her birth village and the caves inhabited by jinn and
sorcerers and the amazing falaj that cut through the village
farms. She had never seen one like it anywhere else.

Then he spoke up suddenly. "I really can't be away from
the house for very long."

She answered quickly, as if he had asked her to justify herself. "My boys are with my friend."

He smiled at her and stood up. She noticed that his phone,
on silent, was signaling a call. She stood up hurriedly. In the
car, the radio was blaring songs clearly but she couldn't understand any of the lyrics. The smell of his hand on her wrist
was a blend of fish and tobacco.

Ghazaala wanted to spend the whole day preparing for her evening date with the Elephant. They were going to the recently opened Mexican restaurant in al-Qarm. But she had barely dropped the twins off at Harir's when her aunt Maliha phoned. As usual, Aunt Maliha's tone of voice ranged from pleading to provoking. "Layla, where are you right now?"

"What do you want, Aunt?" It was her standard response.

Aunt Maliha would not say outright what she wanted. She always began with an elaborate set of preliminaries and made excuses she didn't really mean, mostly about "wasting Layla's precious time." Only after Ghazaala had assured her vigorously that she had the right to take up the time of her brother's daughter would Aunt Maliha say, in a tone of righteous triumph, "I want you to come and pick me up at the Royal Hospital. Take me home. I'm done with my appointment here, and your brothers and your father are all busy."

Ghazaala knew perfectly well that her aunt would not have even tried to phone anyone else first. She was certainly aware of the history: how Aunt Maliha had always refused to learn how to drive or how to take care of herself; of course, she didn't think it was ever suitable to order a taxi. She had consumed so many sugary drinks, first in secret and then openly, that her condition had worsened to the point that now the diabetes threatened her life. But neither the impending possibility of having limbs amputated nor her family's increasing agitation over her state seemed to affect her. She would just laugh, a sly little cackle, a bit like a naughty child caught playing with matches.

Ghazaala asked Harir to go with her on this mission. She couldn't stand it! she said frankly. Not her aunt's grumbling nor her very open pleadings for something beyond help. She hoped that if Harir were there it would encourage her aunt to keep silent. But as soon as she learned—through a rather close interrogation—that Ghazaala's friend was an educated woman like her niece, and was employed, and was a wife and mother, and that her father had been an ambassador before he retired . . . learning all of this, Aunt Maliha began tossing around her typically off-the-wall comments—and in a loud way with rather flamboyant gestures that embarrassed her niece. It really appalled Ghazaala, in fact. Aunt Maliha had a way of saying the wrong thing at the wrong time. Things that were obvious never appeared obvious to her. Her ongoing sense of insecurity seemed to push her into the oddest behaviors. When she was in the company of people she believed to be "successful," she felt that it made her own life look trivial, leading her to stage ever more dramatic and rudely inappropriate performances.

Harir heard all of these interrogations and commentaries with great politeness. After all, this was how she had been raised, thanks to her grandmother's directives in the house by the sea. You always showed respect to those who were older than you, no matter who they were or how they behaved. This wasn't about engaging with a peer or an equal, so Harir didn't feel any discomfort. She even saw the intense questioning to which Aunt Maliha subjected her as amusing, perhaps even natural for someone of an older generation. But she had been slightly surprised to learn that Aunt Maliha was not so advanced in age as she had expected, and that she wasn't unintelligent, either. She was just possessed by a sense of her own victimhood and poor luck.

On the way home Aunt Maliha asked to be taken by the shop. Her manner suggested strongly to Ghazaala that she expected her niece to pay for everything. She did as her aunt asked. No sooner had they returned to the car and Ghazaala had begun to drive than Aunt Maliha declared in a loud voice, "That shop relies on cows to make deliveries." She began laughing and she kept on laughing. Harir looked at her questioningly. Aunt Maliha said, "There it is on the shop sign. Look: You'll receive your order by cow. Bi-baqara!" Startled, Harir called out to Ghazaala, "Back up! Just a little—we want to see what the sign says." Showing her irritation, Ghazaala backed up the car until they were exactly opposite the sign. BI-NAQARA YOUR ORDER WILL ARRIVE. With one click. Two letters that looked alike except for a dot placed beneath or above. A cow or a click? Aunt Maliha just went on chuckling. "Ah hah, I didn't really see what it said, hahaha!" She kept on with her sarcastic comments on shop signs all the way home. "Oh my goodness, a laundry in the sea!" Maliha didn't see the dot over the letter that turned *sea* into *steam*. When Harir tried to correct her, she just cackled on and on. And when they were finally at her address, she got out of the car insisting to Harir that they must see each other again. Ghazaala just took a very deep breath. Her friend laughed. "Take me home now so that I can get on with raising your boys while you go off to your romantic adventures."

Ghazaala drove to the Mexican restaurant. Since the day they'd eaten fish together, there had been nothing to her life but waiting. She was very conscious of that, but she didn't know what she was waiting for.

Waiting—the sharp, pointed teeth of the surgical saw that cuts into one's nerves and sinews. To wait for something, to expect something from this particular person, when you are always conscious that he is another person—an *other* person who dwells inside of his own already settled framework and you have to acknowledge that his portrait inside that frame is already a composition in harmony. You have to recognize, too, that he will not veer from the path he has marked inside those lines, even if he is imagining an ant taking a tiny step-crawl in his path. Given this recognition, there's no choice before you but to be that minuscule ant. In her heart—to her stranger heart—Ghazaala screams: "Don't wait! Don't expect anything!" For nothing is more exact than distances that are measured out, and you cannot become a tiny, invisible ant no matter how strong your desire is to disappear. To hide away somewhere.

She screams in her stranger heart. But the heart is not about to stop and wait.

She screams in this deserted road that she takes. But the road does not listen to anyone.

She screams in the dreams where she sees her own open grave. In his home.

His home, which she does not know. But that home is everything. And you, Ghazaala? You are an ant. Even if your body takes up room enough to move the air a lot more than an ant could.

Ghazaala waited. And she waited. But on this route, in this road, everything is sparse and dry.

If only, instead, to be overflowing! To be an onrush

colliding into the walls of the dam. To be inside the ecstasy of dance where you break your leg. To see dreams as being true and real—spaces where the beloved wells up and fills everything and where you can vanish like a bubble. But what if dreams are, from their very beginnings, simply bubbles? This is a bubble made of mudbrick, its heaviness falling onto her spirit with all of its loud slamming impudence.

Feeling that you love the person who loves you less is frightening. But this felt different: as though Ghazaala were walking down the street when suddenly a car swerved into her. As though her mother, Fathiya, had actually thrown her—had done so with her own hands and arms, and then the bundle had come undone and the baby had been flung hard into the air and remained suspended in the emptiness.

In the Mexican restaurant nothing interrupted their conversation but the noise of crashing plates when the restaurant's regulars flung them against the wall, breaking them as a sign of how much the food pleased them. Ghazaala wondered if people had to pay more here because of the game they were playing—this game of breaking things, which the restaurant seemed to encourage. In the midst of all of this— the quiet of subdued conversation and the tumult of crazy dish-breaking—Ghazaala realized that the Elephant would never flirt with her in the way that the Violin Player and the Singer to the Queen had. With him, there would be no lilting melody, and there would be no queen to fawn over. What, then? A shadow. Here was a shadow bound in chains, hand-cuffed to considerations of the family, his family. What if his son were a playmate of her sons? What if she were to take his daughter to the swings in the park? What if she were to act just as he did, were to imitate him?

He was the man who was already taken, and that was the end of it. But he was the man she was passionate about. She would get up very early in the morning in order to get to the office, because that's where she would see him and keep on seeing him whether he was present or absent. His face would be what she saw and his voice would be all she could hear.

She did think about all of it. This was a lot, she thought. It was too much, in fact. It was sad.

Usually she saw Afraa and her other colleagues before she saw him. For years now, Afraa had talked about her honey-colored wedding. The whole firm knew that she had been di-vorced after less than a year of marriage. But for her, time was frozen; it was suspended within that single moment, the moment of getting married, and she could no longer see any-thing beyond it. No one confronted her about it. The others poured their tea and added milk in the group breakfast ev-ery Thursday, and they inhaled cheese sandwiches, katchu-ris, mandazis, and samosas, and they left Afraa to chatter on about her wedding as if the details of her repeated narratives had become one of the rituals of these staff meals. The leg-endary cake, the wedding planner, the pearl tiara—and this

was Ghazaala's favorite detail because any talk of pearls reminded her of Asiya's father back in the village. In his calmer
moments—she didn't know but she wondered now if he had
been drunk, since when he was drunk, he was meek and trac-
table—he would tell them about half-ruined villas in Abu
Dhabi owned by pearl traders whose glory had faded to nothing and who had lost their fortunes when the pearl trade collapsed. He would sit on the dirt floor of the courtyard, where
there was no longer a Saada or a Zahwa or a Mahbuba or
those goats, and describe one particular mansion as though he
had lived there. It was said that its owner hailed from Sohar.
By 1990 or so, it had been empty—abandoned—for twenty
years at least. But the heirs of the Omani trader refused to
sell it or to even entertain any negotiations over its future.
Asiya's father had been able to slip inside with some of his
army mates. They joked that the soul of the owner would not
object to an evening party held in the ruins of his past glory as
long as the revelers were Omanis whom fate had flung to Abu
Dhabi just as fate had done with him. Even if, for them, fate
had chosen service in the Emirates army, while for him it had
chosen the wealth of the Emirates' pearls. Recounting this,
Asiya's father would flick off the neon lamp in the courtyard
and make shadows with his hands to frighten her and Asiya.
He would tell them that the divers whose lungs had exploded
in the depths of the Gulf would be visiting the mansion at
night. The boat captains who'd been weighed down by debt

would be there and so would the English consul, wearing his dust-laden chest medals. Asiya's father would walk across the courtyard, stooped over to imitate the consul's figure and his gait, and the girls would hoot with laughter. He told them about how the slaves whose backs had been broken by the heft of the pearl caskets would slip out of their graves to come and dance in the sitting rooms of the mansion until dawn. And then, to demonstrate, Asiya's father would dance with jerky movements around the shadowy courtyard in the gloom and cackle at the terror on the girls' faces. "We get old, but they never get any older, they bear their shredded lungs and their broken spines and their dusty petitions of complaint addressed to the consul, and they dance across the floor as they carry them. It's said that a young man and his wife died electrocuted in that villa, and sometimes you could see them still, peering out from the balcony through the cobwebs, because along with the consul and the captains, they want to watch the divers and the slaves dance all night long."

"Did you see them?" Asiya would exclaim.

"Yes," her father whispered. "Their eyes, after the electric bolt hit them, were wide open, and the young man was holding his wife's hand just like I held your mama's hand. Just so . . . just like that." He would squeeze and press his hands together then, and the stories turned into a weave of cobwebs.

14 December 2015

I'm tucked into a corner of the café in front of a cup of black coffee and a slice of date-and-walnut cake, even though I am not a great fan of sweets. I've gotten accustomed to sitting in this same corner, but today I feel detached from the place, alone and outside of time. I am watching myself. I watch myself coming into this café, time after time but always in different guises.

One time I will be *that* sort of woman; I will come in hastily, making a commotion, along with my maid who is carrying the child—the child is heavy, though the maid is very thin and light. Like the other women, I swish in, wearing my silk abaya and sunglasses and clutching my handbag. All of these items, exactly like the other women's belongings, are branded with the names of international designers. The maid will feed the child ice cream, but will she wear a maid's uniform? Pinafore, trousers (striped or solid, in restrained colors). No—it won't go that far. She will be wearing a nice outfit that she selected herself, and I will order whatever sweets she wants. It is not her day off, though; she is here to mind the child. Just as the maids in my father's house never had a day off. Will my son, al-Ayham, feel the same way I felt toward the nannies I had when I was little? These thoughts bother me. It is irritating to find myself defending myself in the exact same terms I would have to use if I were defending these women with their maids and designer brands. I find I'm saying to myself, "She does take a day off every Friday. It's not like the maids of these other women who are forced to consider going on a little outing with their employers as their time off." And then I say, "Self, be someone different."

Or, I will be the exhausted young woman entering this café with my work laptop under my arm, coming straight from the school where I work so that I can deal with some delinquent accounts and have it all squared away before the end of the school year. The income accumulates year by year. People meekly pay their tuition fees, bowing to the legend of private education being better and international schools being the only game in town. Maybe it's not a legend? Maybe al-Ayham will go to this school, too.

The date cake sits untouched on the table. Now, here I am coming in with Daoud, my husband. Here we are, a truly contemporary married couple in a city that is trying hard to keep up with the times. We talk as if we're friends, not lovers. As always, our conversation is quiet and measured. Although whenever my husband starts talking about the falaj system, he can't stop. He is like most academics. It's as if they can never truly leave the lecture hall. Right now he is very busy with some research he's writing up with a colleague on the ancient and famous falaj of al-Awabi. He explains it to me with intense enthusiasm: this is a rare falaj where the local people still use the nightly movements of the stars to allot the distribution of water to the fields, orienting the sluice toward a particular canal and field for a fixed period of time, and then to another, and so on.

He gazes into my face as he speaks, without any pause, as he tells me how sorry he is that this tradition of using the stars is practically dead, as if Aldebaran, relied on in the past, no longer even moves through the sky. He repeats himself. "Practically no one uses the stars anymore, even though in some villages the sundial is still used to tell time." I ask him, "Is it always the same stars?" "Not necessarily," he answers, his zest for the topic obvious. "In other locations, people might use different stars to decide on irrigation times."

Having grown up in a house by the sea, and therefore having hardly ever caught sight of an irrigation canal except as a tourist, I am drawn to this subject. I'm curious, and I'm eager to learn more. I want to know whether all the water in the falaj is owned by the villagers and available for them to use on their own farms. He explains that people do have shares in the falaj, but some distributions have been made into perpetual endowments and the income goes toward repairing the canals as well as maintaining charitable works.

I study him. He is an attractive man, but for me, his intense passion for work is what distinguishes him. If his students at the university don't sense his passion for what he teaches, I would be amazed. Marrying him has given me a sense of what it means to have "stability," even if sometimes I have my doubts as to whether stability is fated for me.

Again I observe myself from the corner in the café. How will I make my appearance this time around? With my father? Will I dare to inform His Excellency the former ambassador of what his long-ago predecessor Sir Henry Wotton said? "An ambassador is an honest gentleman sent to lie abroad for the good of his country." When he told me in Thailand that my mother never really grew up, I felt bewildered, like I suddenly had no words in my head. I had assumed that things might be easier when a person gets married at a young age. The two will change together, right? Why didn't my parents mature in concert?

No, I won't come into the café with my father. I'll come in with my mother—but what will we talk about? My mother is a butterfly. A creature of intense and variegated colors. When she feels like it, my mother puts on a cap of invisibility, just like people did in ancient times, and when she wants to, she summons a flying carpet and takes a ride. The more firmly, awesomely, and even threateningly present her grandmother is—and it's true for my paternal grandmother, too—the more insubstantial, ghostlike, and transitory her own presence becomes.

When I was little I needed her. I still felt needy when I made the trip to Newcastle to study for my master's degree. My father had arranged all of the travel, settling in, and university registration procedures, and then he came twice to visit me. On his own; my mother did not come. I had just recently finished my studies and returned to Oman, looking for work, when she got sick. Transitioning from the stage when I sought support and sympathy in having my mother to the stage in which I provided the support and sympathy was a shock. Did I no longer need my mother because, simply, she needed me now? How would I know that she needed me? Everything—all the signs, the gestures—suggested she needed Josephine and not me, her daughter.

My mother—the woman who blossomed only in herself and only for herself. The badges of honor that marriage confers did not crush her. Among marriage's many heavy burdens, she assumed the weight of only the throne set between her room and my father's. Motherhood brushed her lightly with its wings, as if toying with her existence just for the pleasure of it and no more. Sunata followed by Lakshmi followed by Josephine balanced the household on their heads, and my mother danced on the verge. She grew out her hair but it didn't reach her shoulders, and we joked with her that she looked like Cate Blanchett in *Heaven*. And then we noticed that she really did look like Cate Blanchett. She was only in her forties, but already she was not only a mother but a grandmother.

In the courtyard of the seaside house where we could hear Loza whinnying, we played fattahi ya warda. Open, rose petals! And the rustling sound that my mother's dress made was just as loud, back when she had long hair and the cancer hadn't yet grabbed it away.

I remember that day, when the neighbors' son snatched my brother Faysal's ball and Faysal objected. "That's our ball, we've always had it, we gave birth to it!" My mother wasn't interested in explaining to Faysal that we don't give birth to balls the way we do to babies. She just laughed and ruffled his hair. Those were still the days when I felt a lightness in myself, when I could circle somewhere overhead with my mother, somewhere in the clouds . . . On one day we would play together, and on another I would climb onto Loza's back and whisper, "Loza, my Loza." She recognized the sound of my voice. She knew whether I was feeling cheerful or angry.

And then I lost that sense of being buoyed on the air, of circling in a kind of free state. I never regained it—except that one evening when Asiya put her hand in mine and we walked and walked, around and among the university buildings, Asiya's sharp scent, like the sweat of a gazelle filling my senses. Asiya was the kind of girl who gave the impression that she would protect you. And no one understood that she never had anyone to protect her. She didn't let anyone in on the secret that her conscience was on fire. She burned with it, in silence, and she protected whomever, whatever, she could.

And so, will I see myself entering the café and turning to my favorite nook with this faraway Asiya's hand in mine? Would we share a plate of walnut cake? In that moment, as we turned from the entryway of the university residence into the paths enclosed by dwarf shrubs, Asiya extended her hand toward mine. Was it so that she could snatch me away, or was it to protect herself through me? Which one of us longed for the other's protection as a shield with which you could safely confront the treacheries of the world?

My hand is still and always extended, to wherever your hand is, forever and always scarred by the abrasions of the fingernail on that hand that repelled mine, that body that turned away, forever scarred as guilty by the smoldering pain that words cause.

I saw my hand reaching out. I saw my hand empty. I saw my hands clasped together as if in an eternal prayer. And your hand was not there.

I reached my hands out to you, Asiya. My hands are the soft, pliant leaves of the henna tree. I called out to you. My voice echoes across the wind by way of witches' magic wands. I have waited for you, standing as still and straight as a date palm that has not had water to drink for a thousand years.

And you—what are you?

Your hands—thorns. Your voice—silence. Your still, upright figure—thirst.

How does a person live on words and nothing more? That was who Ghazaala was. Words kept her vital, revived her. Words nourished her. Words were the pivot her life orbited around with unremitting stubbornness.

How had her passionate relationship with words led her to the darkness inside the Elephant's car? She really didn't know. The thread that ran between the definitiveness of the past and the unknown possibilities of the future had frayed, even shredded. Dreams and fancies opened up new combinations—the unknown possibilities of the past versus the definitive future. Every time she dreamed of him kissing her, her own lips seemed to swell and bruise.

In that moment inside the black Citroën, that unpropitious moment, that inharmonious moment when passion is throttled by fear and waiting bows to a hand that is unhurried, a hand that plucks the flowers of one's awaited hopes petal by petal, slowly, deliberately, softly . . . in that moment imprinted with urgency and fear; in that moment, her mind glowed with the memory of the first kiss.

She had made it through her fifteenth year. But it hadn't been easy. As if that year wasn't a span of time that one had to get through, moment by moment, but an unmoving obstacle she had to clamber over if she were ever to reach the magic age, the age Agatha Christie called the year of saying good-bye to childhood. Sixteen!

She was reading Christie's crime novel about the artist who is murdered by his lover with a dose of poison. She identified with the little sister of the artist's wife, who has to bid child-hood goodbye and enter the world of adults. She crouched in the cramped space under the stairs in their building, the book open on her knees, with her math textbook under-neath, since she suspected that one of her parents might poke their head in, even if this possibility was remote given the midday heat. The building in al-Khuwair was a fairly recent construction and it was still mostly empty. There was only their apartment on the ground floor and the Violin Player's on the highest floor, plus the home of an Egyptian family on the floor above them. The smells of frying onions came from the neighbors' as she read how the sister of the artist's wife—whose fifteenth year would come to a close in the novel—was about to become the accused killer. No one suspected the lover, who was the real murderer. They fixed on the teenage girl who was having to say goodbye to childhood with fierce difficulty, in pain.

Suddenly, from her cubbyhole under the stairs, Ghazaala heard the Violin Player's whistle. He was whistling for her. She ran to the top of the common staircase beneath which she had been reading and saw him. From the dusky landing he stepped closer to her. He stretched his arms straight out in front of him as though he were about to gather in and take hold of all the melodies of the world. His palms pressed firmly just under her armpits and he lifted her, stair by stair, until they were on the landing together. He supported her so that she wouldn't drop to the floor, and he kissed her.

It probably lasted only for seconds but her heart kept on pounding like the loudest tabla ever created. As soon as the Violin Player's lips moved off hers, she ran to the staircase and down, down, and out of the building, and through the lanes, dodging around the shops, down the Street of the Tailors and along the school wall, and then she kept on running, running where she didn't know, until finally she collapsed onto the ground. She was certain her heart was about to explode out of its chest-cavity cage and that after today she would never breathe again. She was gasping hard but her open mouth couldn't get air enough to fill her lungs. Barely a year later she escaped from home and married the Violin Player. And one year after that, she whispered to him, "I know I'm pregnant, with you. I felt it and I said to my mother, 'Mama, I'm pregnant.' My mother was so happy! Right away, she broke up some aloe wood into smaller pieces that she put over the coals in the incense burner, and the sharp smell rose around me. She lit the incense. But she didn't know that I was pregnant with you. She didn't know that I know exactly what you would look like, since I have your photo in my wallet next to my ID card."

Her mother wanted to go out immediately to buy tiny white undershirts and neutral-toned swaddling and the cotton slippers that parents put on the feet of both boy babies and girl babies. But her daughter spared her the trouble by announcing that it was going to be a boy. Her mother had a great fund of knowledge about women's bodies and the embryos they carry, and she dismissed Ghazaala's words; it was only the first month, after all. They argued, they both got angry, and the dispute brought back painful memories of her parents' sense of shame and disgrace when she left home to get married without their knowledge.

"All of this, just because she didn't know," Ghazaala whispered. "But I know. I know I am pregnant. With you."

The Violin Player laughed. But his eyes didn't laugh. He brought her closer and kissed her, and she remembered the dimness on the stairs and that first kiss. Was that darkness on the top-floor landing, which was roofed over in wood, in the building in al-Khuwair the same darkness as that in the interior of the black Citroën? And was the Violin Player's hurried kiss on the day she knew she was pregnant anything like the Elephant's kisses? The Elephant consumed her; the Violin Player played a light melody against her skin, and that was all. And so why, then, in this moment that was not propitious, that was not appropriate, was she remembering the half-light at the top of the stairs and a first kiss?

To come close to the Elephant was a frightening experience—something like getting closer than you should to a gigantic waterfall. You knew it was there and you could hear the tremendous sound of its continuous breaking against the rocks. It was there but you wouldn't walk right up to it. That would be too alarming. Once you were that near, if you still believed that you were capable of going farther it meant you had already decided to let yourself shatter on the rocks.

She held him as if she were hugging the wind, and kissed him as she would kiss falling rain, and she looked into his eyes and did not see her reflection there. Where had it gone? Why didn't she see herself in his eyes?

She left the dimness of his car and returned home. Giving the twins a hug, she asked herself, "When will I be home?" Her heart felt shattered; through the long nights she could hear the sound of it splintering. She said to it: "Heart! Get yourself up and out of this abyss." But then it would leap downward as though slipping and falling from the top of a tall building. Vultures tore it to pieces and tossed them far, one chunk in each wadi. During the long nights she said to it,

"Heart, I should not have kept following you like this—you are nothing more than a sightless lump of flesh."

Then she said to it: "And you are deaf, too." But her heart, blind and deaf, didn't answer her. It just left her there, left her behind in the dark passages of its blindness.

Yes, maybe she had touched his skin, but she wanted to touch what was beneath it. Yes, maybe she had breathed in his smell, but she wanted to know the scent of his heart. He said that he knew her, but she wanted it to be a true knowing. She wanted him to wander through her gardens until he reached the most wondrous flora that no one else would be able to find. She sensed his shadow there, in this hurried space, but she did not sense *him*. For haste cancels out the possibility of knowing. Getting to know someone else means a constant renewal. There has to be something new along with a renewal of what was already there for even the flimsiest barriers to crumble. The obstacles will melt away only in the slow and prolonged advance of learning the other—a march that must never come to a stop. If he entered her terrain he would have to cross a great distance slowly, on foot and in patience, without mounting Time, that quickly moving steed. No, he would have to proceed on foot, because he would find branches bending all the way to his hands, questioning his presence, because she would teach him all the names—those names he thought he had learned, when in fact he hadn't.

She complained to him—gently—about the dim close

atmosphere of the car interior and about having only these stolen moments from his family hours. She whispered to him. "You and me—I want the two of us to be somewhere light, with a sky above us, a true and soft blue sky. For you to be my Adam and for me to be your Eve. To be for you. I want you to have your eyes open to the sky and to my heart. I want to see you lying stretched out on the ground, your eyes wide and gazing at the sky so that I can see the sky in your eyes. I do not want you to feel surprised that I have this yearning to know— to search through you, to study you closely, without you stopping me. Because when that happens, it will be the first time that I will really see you. I want to know you. To *know* you."

"Don't be in a hurry about anything," she whispered. "And don't even expect anything in particular. Leave it to me, and let me do what I need to do, slowly. I want to count the hairs in your moustache and the wrinkles in your eyelids. And I want to open up your heart and slay the women of the past who are there inside. It will sadden me if your heart bleeds. I won't ask you to do anything for my sake. No, nothing that would be specially and only for my sake. I won't ask you any questions, because if we don't sincerely believe something in the first place, then what use is it to demand proof? And if we do believe, then proof would be unnecessary in any case. We might start weeping when we recall that this world surrounding us has not yet vanished, that we are not really and truly alone. That our souls are full of torment. We might. Now, though—now . . ."

Ghazaala was determined to tell him how much joy his presence gave her. Even just the thought of his existence in this world made her happy. Life opened to feelings of delight, and she seemed to be walking on ripples of water. This feeling of joy piled upon joy gave her a sense that her body was transparent, a bright form shimmering in the air. She was walking but felt as though she were swimming, or that she was flying when in fact she was making her way through the corridors and along the low glass partitions that separated their desks; flying, and she would come down to land on his desk. She wanted to let him know of this great happiness of hers but he spoke first, moaning about his daughter's condition and complaining about the awful evenings at the hospital. She kept quiet, ashamed to talk about happiness.

"Should happy people be ashamed of their joy when they're in a world filled with misery?" she asked Harir.

"Why would they be ashamed?" asked Harir, sounding startled.

She mused. "Well, these happy people, sure, life has given them their share of misery, but in spite of that they have found some joy. It's as if they are laying claim to the most delicious slice in the cake of life, and it's the slice that others don't even see." She wished the Elephant would say what the Singer to the Queen had said: "I'm kissing strand number 216 in the forest of your hair." But the Elephant never said this or anything like it. The Singer to the Queen was an artist, after all, and the Elephant was not. It was ridiculous for her to toy with these roles in life, to dream of the Singer's delicacy and the Violin Player's fingers within the deep longings of the Elephant, which seemed more like infernal depths, a bottomless chasm.

There was no light in this narrow chasm; the Elephant did not know how to create light. And she was burning.

They tried to stay away from the dark interior of the car. They met in a café. The music was captivating and she whispered to him, "When one is playing music, time has to stop. If it doesn't, the music is meaningless."

He smiled but as if he were scolding her. As if by saying the words *playing music* she was alluding to her ex-husband. His phone lit up. "Why don't you turn it off?" she asked. "I can't . . . my wife . . ." He went silent.

She saw his wife growing larger and larger inside of him.

She was a gigantic figure now, an overpowering figure, and she was growing roots and branches. Ghazaala saw the branches scraping at his skin and tearing it, puncturing it, so that leaves began growing from his hands and feet. She saw him sitting at the head of the table. The large and wonderful family dining table. The sacred table of sacred bonds. She saw herself beneath the table, crouching there and picking up crumbs. She felt horribly alone on a terrible battlefield where she did not want to be. They were sitting at this table in the café, hands interlaced, and suddenly he said, "My wife." And then the palm of her hand was hurting, wounded by the shoots breaking sharply through the skin on his hand. She saw this woman's form extending, stretching upward, outward, still inside of him, growing huge while she shriveled and shrank, with nothing to grow inside of her but him.

"The problem is, my wife worries. She likes to know where I am, it reassures her. I don't want to make her anxious. She's very sensitive and delicate."

"Of course," she murmured. "Of course."

She doesn't sleep. She sees him walking beside her in the streets and sees how their two shadows become three. She senses his hand on hers, and the thorns of the giant tree growing inside of him she can tell are bloodying her. When he talks about "*her* delicacy" and "*her* anxiety," his voice grows gentle and there's a sweetness to it and all the while, as she listens, she is dwindling, shrinking in size. Now she wants to erase her own shadow behind the two of them, she wants to shrink it and find a place for it inside the shadow of the woman who just goes on growing and growing until she fills all of him.

Morning comes. She is less capable than ever of even making a cup of coffee, let alone figuring out how to erase her own shadow. She badly wants to put her own feelings, this turmoil inside of her, into some kind of useful order, but she can't do it. The simpler and more obvious the truths, or the facts, appear to be, the more they seem to expand wildly inside of her, knotting together and blocking her perception. She feels herself knocking into everything around her, because she is guided by a blind heart, even though she has spent months trying to plaster eyes onto her heart. She dug some deep hollows and planted eyes there, so that she could see those plain and simple facts. The sacrosanct dining table that consecrates the sacred bonds. But the eyes remained closed even as the blood welled from the hollows she carved out. She worked a knife blade in there, to separate the eyelids from the skin and to cut away the sticky eyelashes gluing them shut. The heart bled and bled but the eyes were no use. Her blind heart kept on careening painfully into the walls of dead hope and trivial expectations and repeated dreams that were more like nightmares.

In her spells of insomnia she asked herself, "Is this what

passion means?" The music swells from your feet and toes, and lifts you above the ground with its glowing dance. You close your eyes, listening to the melody swirling around you, and when you open them, you have simply collided into the earth's rocky surface and your feet are incapable of taking one more step. You have performed all of the rituals for what is in the end a poor sacrifice, and you have hung your multitude of dressed-up hopes on a fragile, fraying clothesline. You have faced the sharp hard edges of those rocks against your chest, but you didn't die.

He sent her texts: "I am yours." Over and over. As if the two of them had a constant need for this repetition, there in two homes apart from each other, with other people's collars wrapped tightly around the necks of their two souls.

For a brief moment she did think he was hers.

But those collars? The daily tasks and interruptions and responsibilities of a life that would have no grounding without them. Maybe the street between her place and his really was just a street. Not a metaphor, or a barrier, or a forbidden pathway. A street that a car would burn through, that she would easily traverse if she were really and truly "his." But then there would come the realizations, the awakenings. He was not hers. He belonged to those shackles, to the chains he wore.

And she—maybe she was everything. Or some little part of everything. Something of friendship, and serenity, and shelter. A sister's tenderness, a mother's mercy. But what if she did not want to be all of this, what if she didn't care about embracing and stroking his unkempt, sticky life? What if her desire was simply to be his beloved?

That's all, his beloved. With all the gifts of the world and all that history had given, deservedly, to beloveds, all the eagerness and interest and desire, all the big and little things given.

She saw her precarious sense of balance demolished on the threshold of his home. She wanted to regain that self. She wanted some recognition that she deserved to put herself first, if only for a little while. And that she did not deserve all this pain. Had it ever occurred to him how much it wounded her to be running down this path strewn with thorns and neglect, each as harsh and bitter as the next? Did he ever consider her need, in his meager and stingy reality, for some generosity and welcome?

His reality remained stingy and so did hers, but not because either one of them chose it. Even a pressing need, though, didn't seem enough to transform this suppression of choice. Would he ever come close enough to really knowing her before time yanked her away? In a text to him she borrowed words from a poet of their time. "I am the one who arose to break the slate of my future and fate, and when I read your name there, I stepped back. I was intoxicated with my feelings, although what was written there was that you are not mine."

When my mother's grandmother died—as fearsomely matriarchal as ever, her glorious appearance undiminished and her pearls in place—my mother inherited the farmhouse where she had spent her childhood and gave it to me. This way, she said, I would have somewhere to settle down if I ever wanted to return to Sohar. She wasn't persuaded by my "very ordinary" work in a well-known and highly respected school in Muscat or by the idea that I needed any work in the first place. Or by the fact that my husband was not from Sohar and would never settle there. Or by my utter lack of knowledge about running a farm or the inevitable problems over soil salinity and desertification. And she didn't show any more interest in my child than she had shown in us when we were little. My paternal grandmother moved in with us, staying in her old room. Faysal was at college by then, but my grandmother still went into the kitchen every morning to hide the matches high on top of the fridge, just as she had done when Faysal was little and she caught him playing with them one time. After the old gas stoves were replaced with new ones that you could light with an electric spark, she still scolded the cook about the need to hide matches. He explained to her in vain that it was all electric now and he no longer needed those boxes of matches. They argued in a mixture of broken Arabic and Bengali until finally she would return to the sitting room exhausted, repeating to anyone who would listen, "This house would have gone up in flames if it weren't for me." Then Najib would placate her with a plate of sweet khabaisa sprinkled with saffron and dotted with roasted walnuts. She would try hard not to show how much it delighted her. It was her own special way of making it, which she had taught him many years before when he was still an untried young man.

So—Ghazaala talks to me about joy. The most delicious slice in the cake of life, she says, and I try to imagine that mysterious slice, within reach but also too distant to acquire, and I think about my father. Did he ever feel joy in the various cities where he lived? Then I think about my mother. Did she ever feel ashamed, or embarrassed, as she swallowed her slice of cake, or did she swallow it without feeling anything in particular? I think of my mother's grandmother, too. Did joy ever come to see her, like an unknown guest, in the mansion of pearls? I think of my own grandmother, my father's mother, sending shirts as gifts to Najib's brothers in Bangladesh, which made her feel pleased and happy, and about Ghazaala, who says that the existence of her beloved in the world makes her happy every morning when she wakes up. Finally, I think about myself and the young woman on the third floor in the university residence. Was this my joy—the knowledge of her existence and also the mystery, that lure of trying to discover something? I likely hadn't thought about it like this at the time. It was only a few short months in which she appeared and then vanished. I was totally engrossed by her, and that's as much as I understood. Happiness probably requires you to be conscious of it in order to understand and embrace it. As I have gotten older and have seen other people's eyes digging into my life, I have learned to talk about myself in tones of light complaint so that my truly good fortune will be forgiven, or maybe overlooked. With my unmarried colleagues I have remarked that getting married is really and truly a matter of coincidence. If they are married women with no children, I say that children are simply an unending nuisance. With women weighed down by debt, I comment that very soon I will need a big loan of some kind. But my real worries and concerns, which they do not see, I haven't complained about to anyone. Anyway, complain to whom?

Where are those sympathetic aunts people have, who are always liberated and pretty? They seem to be in other women's lives, but that's all I see. My grandparents, my mother's parents, died, electrocuted, not long after she was born. And my father's sisters all succumbed to fever at an early age.

Where is Loza? When I was around nine or ten years old and I got angry at my brothers for teasing me, or my grandmother for rebuking me, I would go to the stable in the yard. As soon as I came in, Loza would come toward me. I would lean my head against the wall and start crying, and she would poke her head close to mine. And when I didn't look at her or work on braiding her mane, she tried to cheer me up in her silent way: she would pick up a mouthful of fodder, which she would drop onto my head and shoulders and then, very gently, she would remove it by taking mouthfuls and eating—or pretending to eat. She would keep at it, her attempts to play with me, until I finally started laughing. I would feed her dates by hand and wait cheerfully for her to spit out the pits, and then I would start clapping my hands.

Then I got older and I went to university. I didn't know that what gave me happiness then was the girl on the third floor, Asiya, who disappeared. I tried everything I could think of to reach her, but it was no use. What if I were to find her now? Would I send her the letter I've composed in my head?

"I've always wanted to write to you but I was too shy, or embarrassed. What did I learn about you, and what did I not know? It was at a time when I thought I knew myself inside out. And then I met you and realized I didn't know myself at all. I hold up the hem of my clothing so that the tractor treads of time won't rip it to shreds. And I dream that one day I will see your face, always composed yet always changing, many faces, wearing a different expression, or a different set of features, each time. I dream that I can read it despite its firm, severe exterior that gives nothing away. As always, I will be astonished at how I am not seeing your face, even though I am looking directly at you—and then, how I see you when I am not looking at you. Your face of many faces, distant faces and close ones. I have wanted to write to you about this intense desire I feel—the need for you to free yourself of the past. About how my breathing is throttled by the hard glint of your finger, heavy against me. I want to write to you, I have a lot to say, but both the sand under my feet and the slippery ice of time passing keep my feet unsteady so that I can't stand firm. I stick out my hands, but your hands are not there to steady me. I have always wanted to write to you, about the horse that looks like Loza that I saw trotting through the university lanes on the evening we walked together, and about the heart with its terrific burden of guilt. I have wanted to write but I have been afraid. I dread having to justify myself, and having to wait, and having to come up with excuses. And, in spite of the enormous things that destroy dreams, I believe in your innocence even if you haven't been able to find any paths to it, and the roads you have had to take have frightened you."

Ghazaala feels she's been put in an annoying position

because her aunt keeps insisting that she wants to see me. I don't understand why Ghazaala feels so irritated, because if Maliha were my aunt then we would moan and groan and comfort each other. She is pleasant, she's fun to be with, and she's open, in spite of her eccentric habits. Or maybe I'm just judging appearances? Things look different to Ghazaala, who criticizes her, who describes her as passive and thinks she needs to learn how to rely on herself rather than always begging for others to care for her. "My aunt exaggerates what it means to not be married," says Ghazaala. "As if, had she been married, she would be a completely different person."

What if Ghazaala hadn't married? I wonder. Would she be the same person? What if I hadn't gotten married? Would I be the same person? What if we weren't mothers? I haven't been comfortable with what Ghazaala says about her aunt. I see it differently. I told her, "You should take care of her." Her answer was: "Do we pay the price of taking care of others by pretending we care? Maybe I'd rather just 'show some interest' when I can, rather than 'taking care of.'" But Ghazaala doesn't take interest in anything outside her own little world—and Maliha isn't inside that world.

I invited the aunt to have coffee with me in my little corner in my favorite café. I was surprised at her nerve, ordering cheesecake—this woman who lives on insulin injections. But there was something about it I found appealing. I ask myself sometimes whether I would find her so pleasant if she were not so completely different from my mother. They are just about the same age. In a tone that was almost a grumble, she apologized that she "wasn't educated" like me. I told her a little bit about my mother, and how she hadn't finished her education, either. She looked at me with a little smile that I couldn't quite decipher. But then she said, "You know, Harir, I was a little girl in the seventies. Al-Waha didn't have that name yet. I used to go to the teacher, Immi Salima, along with all the other boys and girls. We went to her house for our lessons. We all took off our shoes at the door. Since every one of us wore zannubas, and they all looked alike, the way we could tell which ones were ours was by heating up a spoon over the fire and dragging it across the front of the slippers so that the plastic would melt in the shape of the first letters of our names. That's how we all knew our own zannubas."

Maybe she was trying to embarrass me, but I really enjoyed her story. I asked her if she wanted to join the volunteer group I work with sometimes to organize projects. I explained how we decide to work on a certain house, and we work together, young women and young men, to paint walls and put down carpets and arrange donated furniture in the rooms. But she said no. The condition of her health wouldn't allow her to do such things, she explained.

I drove Maliha to the house in al-Khuwair. I was surprised that she fell silent as we went, so I turned on the cassette player and we listened to Salah Jahin. "I fell in love, but it was a love without tenderness; I made friends but it was a friendship without trust."

When I got home, my husband had bathed al-Ayham and put him to bed. I began running through the messages and the photos on my phone. I read Ghazaala's message: "Good evening, Harir. I made a list."

I smiled. Writing out lists was one of Ghazaala's top priorities.

A list of what I will never learn from the Elephant. Here it is:

The color of the bedsheets on the bed where he and his wife sleep. Plain or flowered? Does the sheet just cover the bed or are the ends tucked under the mattress?

The spices his wife uses when she makes the chicken soup he likes best. Does she mix the spices herself or does she buy a ready-made spice mix? Does she buy Nisr spices or Ghazaal?

The way he touches his wife's shoulder or her hand or her back, after he's just been seeing me—does he avoid looking her in the eye? Does he show real attention, does he really touch her and make a big deal about it to hide his guilty feelings? Does he glance at his hands and arms when she's not looking, worried that my shadow might still be there between them? Does he erase my messages as soon as he reads them in case she turns on his phone without warning?

I wrote back. "I preferred your messages telling me about joy, your joy—the sweetest slice in the cake of life."

Maliha dropped the purchased items she had charged to her niece's account onto the chair. It wasn't much—just a few combs, tapes, plastic photo frames, candy, and a few other trivial items that were completely unnecessary. She collapsed onto the bed, panting hard. She slit open the variety pack and lined up all the different kinds of chocolate bars in front of her. Earlier in her life, she had lost the ability to distinguish true hunger from an obsession with eating. When it was combined with a sense of revenge, she could push away both sensations, the hunger and the obsession, and be propelled purely by her desire to avenge herself—on her family in particular, but on the whole world, too, while she was at it. She would inhale as many candy bars as she possibly could. Before she got as fat and flabby as she was now, she had been quite pretty. If someone didn't believe that, they could just ask Suhayb the shop owner. He'd given her a great big wink more than once. Or they could ask the women in the neighborhood. Those women had told her that the men must be dead blind if they didn't notice her. But no man had come forward with an offer of marriage. If she were married, then she would never have had to live this life of hers. She wouldn't have been dependent on her brother, and maybe with her husband's help she would have been successful with the cinema project in al-Waha. They would have shown new films with color trailers, and they would have bought a real projector rather than that primitive machine her brother had found. When she described their operation to the women at the hospital she had lied; it was very primitive. There was no shiny red machine shipped from America. There were no bright yellow English letters spelling out MONARCH. She had seen photographs in a magazine and she made it all up.

Her husband would have called her "my love," like the husband of her brother's daughter, Layla; but her husband wouldn't be anything like that foolish flighty violin player. He would call her "my love" when the two of them were alone, not in front of other people; and he wouldn't leave her as Layla's husband had. She probably would have had children. She did admit to herself that she didn't much like children, and she didn't want to have the responsibility, either, but if she had married it would have been the right thing to do, making it a real family by producing two or three children.

She would have found a maid to help her raise them, and they would then take care of her when she was in her old age. She laughed suddenly, mocking her own thoughts. What old age! This sukkari won't let me live much longer. The thought made her frown. Did people really die of diabetes? In any case, if she had gotten married she wouldn't have neglected her health like this, she wouldn't have ignored this illness, and she wouldn't need to find someone to blame and make them feel guilty for the way her condition had deteriorated. But the fact was that she hadn't married, and no creature on earth would think about her now. If no man had given her a thought on his own then, why hadn't her uncles tried to find her a husband? She couldn't forgive the way they had all neglected and forgotten her.

And then here came Layla with all of the stupid things she said. "Marriage isn't everything, Aunt—live your life." "Learn how to drive, Auntie." "Open a small business, like the shop you had when we were little." "Go and do the adult education courses and get a diploma, Aunt." Didn't this girl who was so full of herself realize that it was too late for any of that? There was nothing left except her swelling body, nothing left except stuffing it with candy bars and insulin jabs.

It was a few days after this shopping trip that Harir had phoned her. But their outing together had deepened the terrible hollowness that Maliha felt inside herself. She had done everything she could to try to demolish this gaping space inside, as well as the chasm she felt between herself and those around her, especially Layla. They were no more than fifteen years apart; yet that girl had graduated from university, while Maliha had barely learned to read and write and do basic arithmetic in Immi Salima's little village kuttab-school. Al-maʿallma, they called Immi Salima. The Teacher.

And then the proper government school was built in Sharaat Bat and the Egyptian teachers arrived. These women were completely different from al-maʿallma. Maliha put them in two different groups. There were those who were getting on in age, and were droopy and fat, and wore the same two or three dresses all year long. Their dresses usually had stains on them, but they hardly ever changed clothes. At the collar you could see a faded nightgown peeping out from underneath; the dress had been pulled hurriedly over it. They always smelled of sweat and fenugreek. They would order the girls to wash the dirty dishes in their kitchen in the teachers' residence and to clean out the fridges that were full of jam jars and rotting food. The other group—they were the young women who always looked cheerful and wore bright dresses and wide belts and elegant heels and had light, translucent scarves from which wafted Qamar 14 perfume. Suhayb offered it at his shop for six riyals. Maliha tried to become friends with these women, who were about her age, giving them little gifts and putting on nice meals. The teachers, who came from Egyptian towns like Mansoura and Port

Said, were hesitant, unsure when faced with the warmth of this village woman. She might be close to them in age but she didn't have a diploma of any sort. But it wasn't long before they overcame their feelings of superiority, which weren't very robust anyway, attracted by the possibility of a few enjoyable hours and some generous hospitality. They made Egyptian basbousa for her, and they taught her how to make halawa paste, from sugar dissolved in water, that they used to remove the hair on their arms and legs. They gave her lessons, teaching her a bit more arithmetic and some elementary science. They moaned about how homesick they were, and about the lovers they had left behind, and their greedy families.

After Maliha left the village with her brother's family, an image stayed in her head of the white wardrobes in the teachers' residence attached to the school. Across the fronts of those wardrobes was written, in bright-colored flowing letters, ONE IS GRATEFUL FOR ONE'S CIRCUMSTANCES.

Layla went to the school that Maliha hadn't gone to. True, Maliha did try to enroll in some adult education classes in al-Khuwair. She could easily read and understand any magazine; she had kept some old issues of *Sayyidati*, the women's magazine. She liked returning to them, studying and marveling over the fashion photos. She could follow simplified explanations of scientific topics. But she did not have a diploma. She didn't know how to accurately describe her feelings of inferiority, but she did have an uncomfortable feeling that her behavior was *crude*. When they became the fashion, she wore those huge bunchy hairpins. She dragged the long hems of her abaya behind her, knowing she might trip over them and that they were likely to pick up a lot of dirt, when this rather extreme maxi length was the going thing. Then, she shortened her abayas up to the anklebone and started wearing running shoes when that became the universal look for university students. But deep down, Maliha knew she lacked the finesse that these other women her age—these educated women—all seemed to have. She knew that however much she followed and tried to keep up with the current trends, and however much more she tried to learn, her rawness would still be there, obvious to everyone in every gesture she made and every word she said.

She was feeling this as she watched Harir sip her coffee. Harir had invited her here, to this fancy café, and Harir had made a show of hiding her surprise when Maliha ordered a large slice of cheesecake with strawberries, but her reaction didn't escape Maliha. Harir's startled look said, "Aren't you having to think about your diabetes?" She didn't care about justifying it, and she tried to eat the strawberries as elegantly as she could. Harir talked frankly and simply about her mother, who was about Maliha's age, and didn't have anything more than a middle school diploma. Maliha thought about how silly this was—Harir's manufactured attempt to

feel what she was feeling, for her sake. Didn't this Harir—
this piece of silk—understand that it was ridiculous to compare her mother, the descendant of pearl traders and the wife
of the ambassador, with Maliha? Didn't she understand that
Maliha knew perfectly well that there are many women in
this world without diplomas who have made their peace with
themselves and who get along fine—but that she was not one
of them?

Maybe this kind of compromise, this peace treaty, was
suitable for a woman born before the seventies, before there
were schools everywhere. But not for her. Or, it might make
sense for a woman whose life in that era had become motherhood and wifehood. But this wasn't her. If only she had not
been born in a village buried between mountains, then she
could have gotten educated. If Suhayb hadn't fled from her,
maybe she would have gotten married. If her brother had not
been such a failure, she would have made the cinema project
work. And there were always others to think about who had
a share in the responsibility for the miserable life she had led.
She didn't forgive any of them. She didn't even feel any leni-
ency toward Harir, sipping her coffee elegantly and talking to
her about joining up with some volunteer charity work.

We decided to make an expedition to see some famous falaj networks. My mother agreed—finally—to come with us.

Al-Ayham insisted on bringing his backpack, which was full of toys, and my mother demanded that we take the teapot, thermos, and some light food. My husband didn't even try to hide his delight at being the tour guide to the places that he loved more than anything.

In the car, Mama was shaking her head, irritated, scoffing at the singsong words on the radio: *A* is for arnab, the rabbit who runs and plays and eats carrots to stay alert every day; *B* is for batta, the duck . . . My husband laughed and said we couldn't change the music as long as al-Ayham was in the car with us. I gave my mother my earphones and my phone so she could listen to whatever music she wanted to hear. But almost immediately she ripped off the earphones and said,

"The aflaj aren't something I have no idea about. We used to swim in them when we were children, in Sohar. Is it true that the jinn of Solomon—peace be upon him!—built the aflaj in Oman? What I always heard was that the prophet Solomon came to Oman and when he saw it was all a desert, he commanded the jinn to build a thousand canals every day!"

Daoud laughed. "No, Auntie. It was people who built these falaj systems. The word *falaj* is found in the ancient Semitic languages, and it means 'a little river.'"

"Aah," she said. "But I haven't seen a falaj anywhere outside of Oman." "Well," said Daoud, "they have them in Iran, Turkey, and China. Some of them go back to the Iron Age; they were renovated over and over as the years went on."

"When do you mean?"

"2700 BC or earlier."

I could hear the sense of pride in his voice. But my mother just put the earphones back on while al-Ayham repeated, "J for jamal fi-l-sahra' . . . a camel in the sands like a ship on the sea." He was still having a bit of trouble pronouncing the S properly.

We reached Falaj Daris: tremendous, beautifully engineered, and peaceful. Al-Ayham jumped into the water and soon found some other boys to play with. Mama was full of wonder at the sight. "Is this falaj from the Iron Age?" Daoud poured her some tea. "No, Aunt. It's from the seventeenth century—the golden age of the falaj. The era of the

Ya'ariba tribal rulers, when agriculture was at the heart of the economy—that's when they got serious about digging canals."

"And Falaj Daris," I spoke up brightly, "is recorded among World Heritage sites by UNESCO." My mother patted me on one cheek. She set the labna and thyme pancakes down in front of us and got up to walk around. I don't know if she was still following a nutritional regimen; she had little interest in food, in any case, and if she was taking any medications, I would not know about it because she would not open up on that subject.

"Your mother is going to get bored with all this talk of the falaj system," said Daoud. "Tell her an entertaining story."

I laughed. "Hah—you're beginning to understand things. Welcome to the family."

On the way to Falaj Khatmein in Birkat al-Mawz Village near Nizwa, I related to Daoud and my mother what Maliha had told me. Her mother had named her Maliha so that she would be as pretty—as maliha—as her mother. She told me that her mother had always told her how the dukhtur proposed to kidnap her, to take her away from home, and he offered her all sorts of promises about what she would have if she agreed to it. But her mother stayed in Sharaat Bat instead, fearful about what could happen to Maliha and her two brothers—her three fatherless children—if she were to leave. She knew well enough that they would be taken away from her protective maternal embrace and dumped into the harshness of life with their paternal uncles. That's why she did not escape the village in the jeep that hovered nearby for several months, circling near their cluster of houses. When the dukhtur finally gave up hope, though, he wasn't stingy with Maliha's mother. He gave her a big sack of painkillers and fever-reducing pills. Perhaps some other gifts as well, but the mother never said anything about them.

"When she told me this"—Harir went on—"I laughed along with her. 'What doctor, or dukhtur, Maliha? If in all of Sohar there was no hospital before the early 1970s, how could there have been any doctors in a remote village like al-Waha?'

"Maliha smiled, and spoke as though she was divulging a great secret. 'He wasn't a real doctor,' she told me.

"'A quack?' I asked. So she told me more. Sometime around 1970, she said, a mysterious and very attractive man appeared in the village with a jeep, some bodyguards, and, it seemed, a lot of money. He settled in Wadi al-Sidr at the foot of the jabal nearby. He put up a long tent and filled it with traditional worked cushions. He hosted festive meals for the people of Sharaat Bat. Once he could see how curious they'd become about him, he told them that he was a physician—a dukhtur—and the sultan had sent him here to treat their illnesses. Then he disappeared for two days. He returned to his tent with sacks full of fever reducers, aspirin, and cough medicines. He opened his tent in the mornings, and people could come; it seemed he studied the girls with a sharp eye. He gave out money and medicine liberally and some nights he seemed to vanish; it was all very odd and mysterious. People whispered to each other that he was trying to seduce their daughters, and indeed even married women, with his gifts, his honeyed words, and his aura. When one of the village men tried to follow him after dark, he pointed his rifle at the man's chest and said, 'One more step and I'll kill you.' The man retreated hastily, and the whispering stopped."

I was ending the story as we reached the falaj. My mother began sprinkling water onto her face, and then she sprayed al-Ayham, who reacted with boisterous laughter. She turned to Daoud. "So, this Falaj Khatmein. Does it also go back to the Ya'ariba era?"

Daoud gripped her hand to keep her from slipping and falling in as we were walking along the rim of the stone saqiya. He told her that after the Imam Sultan bin Sayf ordered the falaj to be dug in 1688, several workers died while digging the main trench and the branch canals beneath the surface because of ground collapses or perhaps from suffocation. "This scared the local people, and they refused to go on with the work. Finally, the imam resorted to making an agreement with the workers. One-third of the falaj water would be theirs and their descendants' in perpetuity. That's how the rest of this hard and dangerous labor was completed."

I wanted to know more about the dangers those workers

faced as they dug these irrigation canals, but my mother was fidgeting. Since she is one of those people who cannot go deeply into anything or take a serious interest in life, my mother doesn't do well with gloomy emotions or too much reflection. The story of the fake doctor-lover might appeal to her, but certainly not a narrative about the diggers of an underground falaj whose walls might fall in on them at any moment.

Ghazaala was sitting back on the white sofa, trying to relax now that the twins had gone to sleep. She picked up the book that had been selected by the book club she had joined with Harir, but she couldn't bring any enthusiasm to it. Not to reading more on the topic of "Why are we so fond of organization and routine in our lives?" She shut the book and turned on the TV, but then she shut that off. She didn't like having the TV blaring in the evening. She realized that she hadn't listened to any classical music since the Violin Player had left her. She wasn't really conscious of it, but she began thinking about him.

After the Violin Player had picked her up, his hands under her arms, on that landing and kissed her, he put his hand out to her and he taught her how to walk. In the distance between her hand and his smile, all roads became passable. Thousands of golden chariots drawn by perfect, beautiful horses rushed forth, all the almond trees blossomed, the birch tree stretched its neck, butterflies fluttered every which way, and mountains moved while streams and oceans overflowed their banks and shores.

She crept out of the apartment just before dawn was breaking. Her mother was already kneading bread dough in the kitchen; her father and brothers would not wake up until the sun was over the horizon. No one would think to look for her, no one would miss her except perhaps Aunt Maliha, who at this moment was snoring in her room, her heavy body turning from side to side but with only momentary breaks between snuffles. Ghazaala flitted out of the apartment like a butterfly herself and found the Violin Player leaning against the front door of the building. They began walking. She had never walked through all of these streets, never seen these open spaces and abandoned gardens and mosque facades, before she had gotten to know him. True, sometimes she would cross through these streets in her father's automobile, but none of it had seized her attention. The Violin Player taught her how to welcome and love walking at dawn, how to discover the city as it was waking up. She watched as Indians living in the city opened their bakeries and tea huts and made egg-and-cheese sandwiches, and she laughed at the school guards stumbling along—at this early moment in their day—still half asleep as they unlocked the gates that had been put in place to protect girls from untoward assignations.

Sometimes he gripped her hand, but if he thought he saw someone's shadow on the street, he pulled away. Sometimes he chatted with her, sometimes he was silent. She was dazzled—by him and by these walks through the city when the sun wasn't quite above the horizon yet. It was still the predawn twilight when he pushed her on the swing in the little garden where most of the swings and benches were falling apart. Then they would run home, hoping to reach their building before her mother had left the kitchen, or her aunt's snoring had strayed from its usual rhythm, or her father had begun his loud humming as he shaved in the bathroom, or her siblings pretended to argue over a few pencils and pens.

After they were married, the Violin Player wanted to take her to the cities where he and his chamber group performed, but she got pregnant very quickly. Then he wanted to take her on big group excursions into the desert with his friends and their wives. But she objected, saying that the twins were too young. What actually scared her was the thought of seeing the enormous fire that was usually lit in such encampments. The sight of big pots swinging over a fire to stew enormous amounts of food always reminded her of the death of Shaybub the cat, when little Zahwa threw him beneath the hot pot over the fire and he couldn't be rescued. Zahwa didn't learn to walk until she was fully two years old. Asiya and Ghazaala took turns carrying her. That was what led to their final expulsion from the games of hide-and-seek the boys and girls in their village played every afternoon after school. You had to be able to run and to hide. Carrying a heavy toddler slowed them down, and Zahwa's shouts and screams made hiding impossible. Finally she started walking, and then anything that fell into her strong grip was doomed—a bird throttled or a toy torn apart. She had already learned by watching others to scurry over and throw whatever it was into the rubbish bin, or into the falaj, or somewhere else. On that day, her father was preparing a feast for his neighbors, making a meat broth in the large pot in the courtyard. He didn't see it, but Zahwa picked up Shaybub and threw him right into the flames.

It must have been nearly dawn by the time Ghazaala fell asleep on the sofa. When she woke, she felt sluggish, weighed down by some dream. She didn't have time to recall any of the details and ponder them. She woke her two sons, made their sandwiches, took a shower, and in under an hour she was on her way to work. It was nearly the end of the month. She had to pay the bills and justify the account books—expenditure and income—and check bank statements to verify that they were accurate.

After her morning break she went to the company's IT office. Her colleague Mazin shook his head when he saw her coming. "Layla, give us a little time, c'mon, sister! We haven't put the schedule together yet." She sat down across from him. "Mazin, my brother, I'm just here to ask whether you've got all the data together, and—" But Mazin (whom everyone in the company knew as Mazin al-Kharrat, since he bluffed everybody about everything) just poured her a cup of tea from a thermos he had at the ready and drowned out her questions by going on and on with his usual little speech about all the gold that was hidden in the huge palaces of Muammar Gaddafi. His brother, he told her, had traveled to Libya on his own and had unearthed some of it. The problem was trying to get the treasure out of there.

She took one sip of tea and got to her feet. "Mazin, the proposed budget—all the data has to be ready and available for input into the system I'm working in—it's got to be all set for the start of the month. I'd really like to have as few random figures as possible and also to reduce necessary paperwork. Can we agree on this please?"

Mazin twisted his lips and muttered something as she was leaving. "Divorced women. Even Afraa—she's divorced, too, but she isn't as nerved up as you are."

Before the workday was over she went to the Elephant's office. She was thinking about all the hours and days that had gone to waste because she had not been with him, about so much of her life having passed by without them together, about what value life would hold if he were not in it. If she couldn't breathe in the same air he breathed, she would suffocate. But the air he breathed was vowed to another.

"This love makes no sense." That's what Harir told her.

"Does grace make any sense?" Ghazaala asked in response.

At the sight of her the Elephant was clearly flustered. He turned his head this way and that. Why couldn't she have fallen in love with a man like Harir's husband, someone practical, always self-regulated, and open? Someone who would be a "friend," which is how Harir described her partner. The whole time she had known the Singer to the Queen she had thought of him as a close friend, although his tendency to make everything about himself hampered his ability to really be anyone's friend. She had thought that her husband the Violin Player was a friend, but then it became obvious that she had not understood him at all. So what about the Elephant? The way her blindness swept her away when it came to him meant she had no idea. Did she want a lover or a friend? Harir would say that friendship was more important and longer lasting than love, but Ghazaala was aflame with the idea of love. Love precisely; love first and last.

Anyway, why did Harir always make so much of describing her husband as a friend? Did she want to hint—maybe even unconsciously—to Ghazaala that her marriage, as much as it was an utterly conventional one, was more lasting than the love match Ghazaala had made? Or did she want to minimize the issue of passion for the sake of preserving some stability in her relationship? Ghazaala resented her friend's implied criticism of her life; she thought Harir was wrong.

But she kept her rebuke to herself, repressing it, an ongoing source of sadness in her spirit.

Now she tried to start a conversation with the Elephant about ordinary things. About work. She told him about the scheme to develop the statistics used on the balance sheet so that they could compare the budget more easily to actual expenditures. But he continued to look discomfited at her presence here in his office.

She observed him sitting there across his desk from her. She saw him trussed and bound, choking on the strings attached to him, woven round him by family needs. When he stood up, he was batting his arms about and shifting his feet as if trying to ward off a netting of cobwebs. As if the spider's strands were winding themselves round him and he could not find a way to get free. She saw him pacing, but his steps were broken as though he remained moored in one place, shackled by duty and fear and responsibilities. How could she have ever seen him as a free man, which is what he had looked like to her before she had grown closer and learned to see the webs and ties? How could a family cast a man in this cement straitjacket so that he could no longer see himself? Every way he turned in life only led back to this rigid cement-like frame. One time she teased him about it. "Is your wife happy with this dedication you show, this total consecration to your family?" "No, she's not happy enough," he said, "because she sees me making less effort than the husbands of her sisters and friends." Was this what the Violin Player had fled from, years before? A cement straitjacket?

Returning home, she felt tormented by her curiosity to see this woman who was able to attach and manipulate all of these strings and who could keep this tune of insufficiency and guilt on a constant playback loop going around and around inside of him. She went through his Facebook page until she finally found one photo. He was standing to the left with his arm around his wife, the palm of his hand resting on her shoulder and the other hand on the boy's head. The girl was standing in front of her mother—blank narrow eyes, pointy teeth, and a wide grin. Despite the boy's composed features and the father's hand sunk in his curly hair, he looked wary, ready to leap out of the picture at any moment. She saw anxiety in the father's eyes, competing with his strained smile. The wife was looking at the camera but the lights seemed to have gone out in her eyes. There wasn't the slightest glimmer of a passion for life in those eyes. It was as though this woman had stood unmoving next to the anxious husband, the wary, poised boy, and the afflicted girl for so many long years that time had sucked the spark of life from her gaze little by little. They were all wearing nice, even fancy, clothes; perhaps it was a special day. The only person in this family photograph who seemed at peace with the world was the girl, who was the cause of so much anxiety and pain but whose cheerful play was oblivious to it. There was no life in this picture, no sense of fun or joy except in the girl, who was completely unaware of being the source of all of this grief. And Ghazaala didn't see anything of her own shadow anywhere in the photo—just as it didn't exist anywhere in his life, a life with no room for shadows. She stared at this girl who had been born with Down's syndrome. Amina— the Trusting, the Trusted. She saw true joy and peace in that face. She shut her laptop, turned off the lamp, and went on sitting there in the dark staring at nothing in particular. Suddenly, inside of her there stirred her husband's voice, her ex-husband, the Violin Player. "Is this life?" he was saying.

Ghazaala had been in her third year at the business college. She had chosen to specialize in accounting, as Harir had done. Dealing with the children, the nursery, the university, and the supermarket consumed her day. Her twins' birthday was coming up and she wanted to invite children from the nursery and her friend Harir, and perhaps a few other classmates. She spent the day before the party shopping: gifts, balloons, party hats, streamers, chicken nuggets, boxes of juice, cake. She spent the day blowing up balloons, hanging the party decor she had bought, frying the nuggets, recording the right songs, and laying tablecloths. She spent the evening cleaning up after she bathed the boys, who were bouncing around delighted with their birthday presents.

Tired out, she threw herself into bed. The Violin Player was lying there, his hands clasped beneath his neck, still wearing his striped gray shirt. Without turning toward her, he mused, "Is this all that life has to offer?" She was truly exhausted and she didn't even try to understand what he was getting at. She was so sleepy she couldn't keep her eyelids open as she heard him saying, very slowly, "This eternally spinning top of family harmony—is this life? And putting on boring parties that require a lot of work, and following feeding schedules, and putting away colored pencils and broken toys, and shopping for household needs, and making family visits because one has to make family visits—is this life? Is this eternal routine what I want from life?"

Ghazaala fell asleep and had a dream. Life appeared as an enormous spinning top. Stuffed toys were flying every which way, balloons were popping, broken pencils lay scattered across the floor, and children were throwing up. And the Violin Player stood at the center, laughing derisively.

I was with Ghazaala at the Trade Center. Al-Ayham was with his father, and Ghazaala's boys were with us. "What about going to see the new Disney film?" I asked. "Since we have your boys." But she objected. "Ever since the Swedish Iraqi told me, with a lot of sarcasm in his voice, about how his artist friends were going in droves to work at Disney and the other big film companies so that they could be sure of having a good, steady income, I've had a certain aversion to the idea of seeing any Disney films."

"Do you have a problem with good, steady income?"

"Hah—no. But he also told me that a lot of the films produced by Disney aren't originals anyway. What he said was that some of them plagiarize from Japanese anime."

"I like Disney films. They're clever."

"But like most American films, they are soooo predictable, and they always uphold the same old values."

In the end we chose a different film. As we sat there, I couldn't concentrate at all. My husband had taken al-Ayham to play electronic games, as usual. He was the one who always took the boy to entertainment places and ice cream shops. He was the one who made sure al-Ayham brushed his teeth before going to bed and drank his milk in the morning. My husband thinks I'm an insensitive mother. He can't see that it's natural for the maid to bathe the boy and get him dressed. I told him that I was always fed and dressed by servants, all my life, and it didn't hurt me. He answers that he cares about the daily details of our son's life more than I do. Maybe he's right. But a lack of concern is the only model of motherhood I ever experienced. I'm probably not capable of constructing any other model. Or maybe I just wasn't created for family life. For what, then? Being on horseback?

There had been a horse farm in Sohar. For several years, a wooden sign posted on its metal fence announced TRAINING IN HORSEMANSHIP. It wasn't a school; it didn't even have a name. When I began going round there, my horse, Loza, had a mysterious disease and couldn't walk or run. So I made some attempts to get along with new horses and with the trainers who worked on that farm. They weren't from the area. I might now be a true equestrian if events hadn't interfered—events that collided and formed such a towering hurdle that it would be impossible for my life—if my life was a horse—to jump over it. But now I don't even really know what it was that stopped me. Was it my paternal grandmother's grousing about me, a girl, learning to ride horses? She said there were "well-known dangers" when a girl started riding horses. Even though my father didn't pay attention to what she said on most matters, her constant complaining about this one cast a dark shadow over my riding lessons, and her muttered warnings put major obstacles in my path. Then the Training in Horsemanship farm was suddenly shut down and the trainers vanished. And then Loza died. So the horse of my life came to a dead halt, stopped by an impossible hurdle.

The day after our trip to the Trade Center, I was in my office working in a perfunctory manner. The program coordinator summoned me. "Harir, come to my office—I have ordered a coffee for you."

I sighed. "Thamna, the coffee you order is very bad and you know it."

She laughed. "It doesn't matter. What matters is that it is very pricey."

I gave in. "Let me close this account, and I'll come."

I walked over to her spacious office. The table overflowed with photo frames and cards and trophies. Behind her was a life-size portrait of the sultan. Her office always smells like precious aged incense; I sniff and I can't hide my reaction and she laughs. "Smell, smell—you northerners don't understand what real incense is." I take the large cup with my name written on the front. "At least we understand coffee," I say.

At that, she began laughing so hard that her full body was shaking, and she gave me a wink from one of her heavily kohled eyes. "Enough—come and see this lovely lady who wants to present her workshop for the school."

I toyed with the cup, having no intention of drinking from it. "A workshop on self-development, I suppose?!"

She patted her blond highlights. "Of course. It's the going thing. Should I respond to her honestly, or officially?"

I laughed. "Let me hear the honest response."

Thamna straightened her back and lifted her head and slowly lowered her artificial eyelashes. "My dear self-development trainer, I regret to inform you that our fine school doesn't permit workshops unless the people who run them are foreigners. It is especially preferred that they have light-colored hair and blue eyes. Since these characteristics are not applicable to you, bye-bye."

To show me that these characteristics indeed were not applicable, she turned her computer screen so that I could see. The image there seemed very familiar even if I didn't recognize it immediately. I read the name and title beneath: development trainer, with international credentials, Shuruq Ahmad.

Shuruq—my roommate back at university. She still looked something like her younger self despite the multicolored shawl, the tinted hair, the blindingly white teeth, and the nose that had seen cosmetic surgery, probably in Iran.

Thamna returned her screen to its usual position. "Never mind that. Guess how much I made my husband pay for this bracelet. Hah—what's wrong?"

I stood up. "Thamna, I have to get back."

She tossed her head. "To your office?"

"No," I said. "To the horses."

Aunt Maliha planned meticulously for her own death. The days of compulsory mourning that would follow it, she figured, would amount to her true victory. They would be days of punishment for her family, and this would make her revenge against them complete. Maliha wanted to imprison her family within her death; she wanted their lithe and playful bodies to disintegrate inside of her infirm, swollen, neglected body—the body whose death was consecrated to punishing the life in theirs. She would die, and finally they would be forced to think about her. They would all gather— and it would be because of her. They would abandon their important preoccupations, their jobs, children, and friends, to come together, submissively, for the necessary performance of the mourning rituals. No one would escape the throttling grip of her death. They would be forced to weep and to speak about her to all the other mourners in attendance. They wouldn't be able to overlook or neglect her then: she would be the focus of their attention, the person they couldn't shrug off. She would be in front of them through every moment of it, the pivot around whom they would circle as they had never done in her life.

Her mad brother would come from al-Waha, his hair long and his beard neglected, finally realizing after all this time—after it was too late—that if he had involved her in his projects, the ones he attempted after the failure of the cinema, then neither of them would be in the state they were in now, at the end of it all. He would regret that he hadn't kept her beside him so that they could take care of each other like proper brothers and sisters do. He would recall the rare moments of joy—like when she was taking the tickets for the cinema, chuckling because no one could watch the film without getting by her first. Yes, he would feel regret. In fact, he would be weighed down forever by the heavy burden of regret bestowed upon him. He deserved it all, for ignoring and neglecting her.

Her elder brother, retired from the Housing Ministry, would have to leave the café where he sat playing cards with his friends every day and come to sit in mourning. He would no longer be able to do what he had always done: walk by her room in his house, pretending it didn't exist and neither did she, or talk to her only when absolutely necessary and in an incomprehensible mumble. No, he would have to say things about her and he would have to say them clearly and respectfully for those who were there, like any proper elder brother would do. The paltry sum of money that he doled out to her in clear irritation each month—from the rent on their father's farm, which they had inherited—he would pay many times that amount now to cover the expenses of the funeral and the mourning period, where so much food and coffee had to be supplied, and he would listen to people saying prayers for *her* after they had eaten up *his* money. What a victory, how glorious! Did he really think she didn't know that he had taken bribes in exchange for greasing the wheels for certain people when he was still at the ministry? Did he consider himself a respectable man? Was there any respectable man who would receive his daughter in his home after she had run away to get married in a court? He had even held a wedding for her, afterward—how shameful was that! Anyway, he would have to sit there, mourning his sister. Imagining these moments made Maliha so deliriously happy that she almost wanted to dance—if only the diabetes hadn't rotted her feet, and would soon do her in completely, making her dreams of revenge come true.

And Fathiya, her brother's wife—how she enjoyed imagining Fathiya forced to sit there mourning her, in her own house. This was the house where, from the very start, Fathiya had gone to such lengths to exert her control over everything. She did her utmost to dictate how Maliha would be treated—at best, as an unwelcome guest; at worst, like rubbish that wouldn't fit in the bin. In death Maliha's neck would grow loose and stretch, and it would be Fathiya who would have to stoop over it to wash and perfume her body. She might even have to hear the neighbors gossiping about how she had neglected her husband's ailing sister: music to the ear of the dead woman. The neighbors would whisper their insinuations loudly with knowing winks. Couldn't Fathiya have cooked nutritious meals for poor Maliha? Medicine came free from the government, so how difficult would it have been for Fathiya to actually watch and take care that she had her medicine on schedule, and to give her the insulin injections—poor Maliha, who hadn't been blessed with sisters or daughters—rather than abandoning her and letting her condition worsen until she had to have a foot amputated, and then died? The more they hinted, the more Fathiya would be forced to endure the torment she deserved—now that her crime against Maliha was out in the open. And her daughter—that spoiled, misguided, wayward girl. Why, when Layla had to sit there mourning her aunt, she would realize that she had committed an unpardonable sin by failing to invite Maliha to come and live with her after her divorce. That corrupt husband of hers had seduced and deceived her, and then he had left her—when she was a mother and a working woman! But she turned her gaze away from her aunt's wishes to come and live with her and take care of her children. That misguided girl preferred the nursery over the nursing of her aunt. But now she would have to leave those darling boys and come to mourn her aunt. And her brothers—so taken up with their car races and silly trivial games, they would be sitting in the majlis for their aunt's mourning and they would have to be polite for hours on end. They would carry her heavy coffin on their weak, silly shoulders, bending meekly under the weight of her. Yes, all of them would be there, a little crowd of them, and all for her sake. Maybe there would be a procession, men and women in mourning in a line stretching all the way from al-Waha to al-Khuwair, coming especially for this day of remembrance. Maybe those people would be remembering her childhood and her teenage days. How fervently she hoped that in their devotions they would make some room for curses against her uncles, who hadn't cared enough to find her a husband or send her to school somewhere other than al-Waha, as they had done for her two brothers. All they did was send her to Immi Salima's kuttab-school to learn some elementary reading and writing. Her father had died when she was still nursing at her mama's breasts, and then her mother had died—all of it before either parent had her long enough to pour their love into her. All so sad! If the two of them had been forced to witness her death, if her parents had to attend the days of mourning, then her happiness would be truly complete.

With her death she would seize all the power that life

had never given her. There would not exist, on the face of this earth, a happier or more fortunate corpse, when people gathered around her inert form as they had never gathered around her live body. If corpses could laugh, hers would never stop cackling. She would mock them forever, eternal laughingstocks.

24 March 2016

I stood at the stable door studying the sign hanging there. ZINAT AL-JIYAD LIL-FURUSIYYA. THE MOST BEAUTIFUL MOUNTS FOR SUPERB HORSEMANSHIP. "Perfect," I breathed. I remembered joking with Maliha about "names that are the wrong fit," as she had put it. Names on signs like EYELASHES OF THE EVENING FOR QUR'AN MEMORIZATION or THE MODEL OF RECTITUDE FOR SATELLITE DISHES or THE FIFTH-GENERATION KUSHARI NOODLES. These signs amused us so much that Maliha made me stop the car so we could take pictures. That was before she stopped going out with me, or going out of the house at all, as Ghazaala told me was now the case.

I entered the stable and the smell of the horses surrounded me. Enclosed me. My pulse raced—I felt as though I were walking into my own dreams. The woman I found there welcomed me. This trainer looked about my age. Her name was Shiyam. She let me wander around as much as I wanted. I went to the show horses' section. They were all Arabians with known pedigrees. Another young woman, wearing riding clothes, was whispering into the ear of one as she braided its mane. I stood next to her staring at the gorgeous white stallion. She turned to me and said, "This is al-Rayyan, he's the king of competitions." She pronounced his name merrily but nearly in a whisper, as if she were revealing the name of her beloved that she had never told anyone before. "I'm Harir," I told her. "I came for some training." She put out her hand. "I'm Suhaila. I came here after a very difficult time in my life."

In the packhorse section, the animals were more heavyset, closer to Loza's form. Their coats were mostly shades of russet. I studied them, one by one, until I saw him. And I felt some sort of recognition. This was the horse I wanted to ride. Shiyam laughed. "Barq. Lightning! He's stubborn and unruly; we don't advise beginners to try him." I stood my ground. "I'm not a beginner. I just had a long gap."

"He's just come back from the track. It's time for his bath."

"I'll bathe him," I said immediately. Together we led Barq out to the open area. I hosed him down and rubbed him gently with a special loofah before drying him off with a towel. Shiyam watched as I tried to communicate with the horse. We led him back to his berth so he could rest and perhaps doze off. But I couldn't leave him. "This is the one. I will ride

Barq, not any of the others." The trainer smiled sympatheti-cally. I sat down, leaning my back against the wall to the right of the horse. "You are so beautiful!" I whispered to him. And then I seemed to doze a bit, too.

I woke to the sound of children's voices coming from the open area. Likely, they had finished their riding lessons and were getting ready to leave. I opened my eyes; Barq's eyes opened, too. We looked at each other and I told him about Loza.

Suhaila came over to me. "You are just like me."

"Why?" I was very surprised.

She smiled. "Because you are passionate about horses."

I laughed. "Really? How did you know? I don't even know that. It's been years."

Suhaila leaned against the wall as I was getting to my feet. "How could I not know? Horses are the love of my life."

I remembered what she had said as she was whispering to the Arabian stallion. "Why are you here, and after a really hard time?" I asked her.

She scooped up an armful of straw and set it down in front of one of the horses. "This one is Rajih. He has a particular thing about eating. Aah, Harir, all sorts of things happened to me before I could get to this place—to a place where I could spend all day every day in the stable helping Shiyam. You know? If Shiyam asked me to pay to work here instead of being paid, I'd agree to it.

"I was little. I saw horses for the first time ever in Al-Sahwa Public Park in Sib. I rode, just in a little circle like the other children, but I went crazy over it. My father enrolled my brothers in a riding school, but he refused to let me go with them. He said I was too old, it was wrong, it wasn't respectable for girls to ride horses. Especially since the trainers were all young men. I saved up my school allowance and bought a helmet and riding breeches from the tack shop. My father found them and threw them away. I cried and sobbed and begged but it was no use. Then I was at university and I began riding at the university stables without telling my father. I fell in love with my trainer but he deceived me; he left me to marry his cousin. We had a fight in the stables, in front of everyone, and he threw me out. My family found out about it, and my father ended my university studies and locked me up at home. I got ill and I had such a fever that I was raving, calling out the name of my favorite horse. Layl. My mother was very worried and afraid for me, and she promised I could go back to riding if I got well. So I did. But she couldn't keep her promise. My father made me swear on the Qur'an that I would not go near the stables in exchange for being allowed to go back to my studies. I started seeing Layl in my dreams. I graduated and I met Shiyam. She and her husband had started this stable to train girls in the morning, and he trains boys in the afternoon. This was the magic solution for me. My father has begun to relent, finally, especially since I can bring in more money helping train little girls and boys and older girls than I could make in any other job."

She threw Rajih another fistful of straw and then turned back to me. "Now I'm in my own paradise here, after all of the suffering."

The next morning at 6:00 a.m. I was on Barq's back. I hadn't forgotten how to do this, as I had thought; I just needed some additional training and some work to learn proper dressage. Barq and I became like one being, as though he were an extension of my body and as if our harmony had always been there.

Then I brought al-Ayham with me. Suhaila was charmed by him. She chose a cute mare for him and encouraged him gently. I couldn't suppress my fear, but al-Ayham didn't fall off once. He was a quick learner—how to steady his little body and keep himself in the saddle. His long hair flew about as he squealed happily. He rode by himself and sometimes with me. I could hardly believe it—me, who thought I would never be able to escape the fate of my mother with her lack of maternal emotions. Me, who thought that there was no hope, that I would never find a way to share something with my son—here we were, both of us totally in love with riding our horses, a joy we have shared day by day and minute by minute.

Zinat al-Jiyad brought me back to the essence of who I am, and it brought my son back to me.

Harir, did you know that in this formidable school, one of the conditions for acceptance used to be 'perfect physical condition'?" Thamna asked me. "Listen—my uncle was top student in his year at his school in the south. A delegation from this school traveled to all the local schools to pick the top students for scholarships and board—this was in the 1980s—but they refused to enroll my uncle because he had a slight eye muscle problem in his right eye."

She had a little splotch of her dark red lipstick on her teeth. "Where is your uncle now?" I asked.

She laughed. "He runs three private schools, they're our competition."

"Why didn't you go to work for him?"

"Ooh, Harir, just look at me. I am 'in perfect physical condition'—I'm here to get our revenge."

We laughed, making light of it in defiance of the teary

wandering eyes of children, the archive of the past. I suggested she come with me and Ghazaala to International Village to shop. She agreed.

Ghazaala waved at the huge statue that had been erected at the entrance to the America pavilion and laughed. "Look, Harir, the cowboy stands there as the whole world walks by and has to duck under his trouser legs." I tugged at her hand. "Come on, let's go to the Africa pavilion. Thamna and I want to buy some masks." But she led us instead to the Turkey pavilion; she just wanted to go into clothing shops. She was gazing at the nightgowns—their sheer material, the lace and bits of silk—and stroking the soft fabrics with both hands and repeating as if she wasn't aware of what she was saying, "I just want to be his and I want him to be mine." I gave her a little shake to get her away. "This is madness, Ghazaala. He's married." "If he would just look at me, *really* look at me," she sighed, "I think it would be enough to make me pregnant. He would give me a child. Maybe twins again." If her work colleague became hers, would she wash his hair and cut his nails and spoil him the way she did the Violin Player? "True, someone can be in love more than once in their life," she had told me. "But it's not the same love—not at all."

She led me to another shop, where she showed me a bright red nightgown. I was embarrassed. "This is what I'll put on for him," she said. "He loves red." I hid my chagrin with a laugh. "Why? Is he a bull who's maddened when he sees red?" Ghazaala whispered to me as the nightgown, which she would never wear, slipped from her fingers. "No, he's an elephant."

Fate decreed that I would meet her beloved a few months later. He wasn't an elephant. He was a man of medium build and ordinary features and a humdrum voice. There was nothing extraordinary about the way he acted. He phoned me at my office and asked to meet since I was her close friend. He was hoping I would understand and would respect his position. I didn't want to meet him in any public establishment. We met in the car park of the school where I work. I wanted to make it clear to him that I do not interfere in any of Ghazaala's business no matter how much I may disagree with her. But he didn't give me an opportunity to say anything. He told me what he wanted to tell me, without taking a breath until he was finished, as if he were trying to fling away a heavy load. "I'm grateful to you, Harir, that you are here listening to me. Layla thinks I don't pay any attention to her, she thinks I don't care, and maybe she even believes I deceived her about my interest. Even worse, she may think I lied to her when I told her I loved her. To be honest, I don't know what she thinks, because she hasn't let me know anything. Since I began avoiding talking to her and refusing her hints that we go out together, she hasn't scolded me, but I can see her losing her sparkle. I didn't deceive her, Harir, and I've never in my life known a woman like her. But when we met, it was already too late. I am not a free man. My wife is my cousin, and she grew up in our household as an orphan. I've always been the focus for her. She sees the world through my eyes and sees me as the world. And we've had the terrible weight of having an invalid daughter who requires all our attention and time. I'm a man with a heavy load to carry, responsibilities, and now a sense of betrayal—it's already unbearable. My family isn't to blame for my love. Aren't they the ones who most deserve my care and my time? If everyone ran after their hearts, think how many destroyed homes there would be. You, Harir—you have a family, you understand this. Probably Layla understands it, too, but she has been shattered. I don't want to crush her even more, but I want her to wake up to reality. Why does Layla always give the appearance of living on another planet from the rest of us?"

"Her name is Ghazaala," I said. The Gazelle.

What he told me seems like such an old and threadbare story. As if, precisely because it is so ancient, no one wants to hear it anymore. This old love story. This ancient story always follows the same slippery slope. Attachment or needing to cling, waiting and expectations, the impossibility of sleep, then doubt and suspicion, and finally despair. As old a story, truly, as there can ever be. The painful, shocking affirmation that at their core people are always alone—and it has to be recognized again and again, every time love fails, as it must do, to unite two beings who are essentially separate and alone.

Ghazaala pushes her world in front of her like a huge and heavy chest without wheels, and this man drags his world behind him—the train car that has all but flattened him beneath its wheels. The heavy, solid chest collides with the train car. Some objects are scattered and destroyed, and what is already defective is weakened even more. She binds her heavy chest onto her shoulders with rope. No matter that it may destroy her bones. In front of the train car, the man tries to keep himself balanced by performing acrobatics. No matter that the contortions might shatter his backbone. What matters is what the two of them agreed upon. That the collision not ruin what the two of them are carrying.

He wants to emerge from this accident sound, safe, and whole. Ghazaala knows that she will not emerge. I began walking faster, toward the school. The morning line of students was almost all in and I was supposed to be in the finance office by now. I tried to work on the bills and figures but one nightmarish image ruled me the whole day. Ghazaala in this man's embrace while he was telling her that he loved his wife.

We met at her new house; she had recently paid off the mortgage. Her sons had left their game in the neighborhood to come and teach al-Ayham more soccer skills in the garden. From where I sat on the balcony with Ghazaala, I could hear his shouting, ecstatic that these older boys were paying him some attention. She put her coffee cup down on the tray and asked me suddenly whether I had ever felt outside of myself, removed from time and place. This is Ghazaala—not interested in firm ground or hard realities. Rather, she's focused on shattered feelings and how we all use our memories to serve our own particular needs and aims. I closed my eyes and thought back to Asiya: the flutter of her abaya, the veins on her hands as she gently grasped my shoulders, her eyes asking me why I was following her. I took her large hand in both of mine and almost kissed it. Then we walked hand in hand between the wings of the building, through the corridors, around the inner courtyard to the residence entrance, and then up and down the small lanes inside the university precinct. Around the colleges, through the faculty residential compound, and around the grounds that were bare except for scrubby bushes. I could almost hear the blood pumping through the veins on her hand that was now closed around mine. I was breathing in her sharp smell and trying to match her stride. She was walking like a person shaking off all of life's pressures and shrugging off people's opinions, whatever they might be. There was something dark here, something not to be revealed. Something disturbed, and disturbing, repressed, caged somewhere inside. Those were the hours in which I felt like I was nowhere, like I was not inside of any place or time. As though I were on Loza's back and she was running along the seashore, far, far away; the shouts of the trainer were no more than distant echoes and I was flying with Loza.

Did I talk to Asiya? If so, what did I have to say? I don't remember now. As for her, after a very long silence she told me one story.

"One day a baby girl was born who was more beautiful than anything in the world. Her parents were crazy about her. She had a sister who was about eight and was eaten up by her burning desire to regain the love that was now entirely focused on the little one. When she was three years old, and her parents doted on her more than ever, this beloved child threw her sister's cat into the fire that was lit beneath a huge cooking pot in the courtyard, preparing for a feast. The cat moaned and cried, like any person would, until he died. No one blamed the beloved little girl; they blamed the older sister for letting her get too close to the fire. In her bitter-tasting mourning for the cat, the older sister stood at midday on the rim of the falaj. Her tears fell into the water and she watched their final sparkle as they disappeared beneath the surface . . . The beloved child had followed her and was tugging at her clothing, wanting to play. Finally the older sister gave her a push, and she toppled into the canal and the current carried her away."

Ghazaala gave me a shake. I opened my eyes. They were wet. "Outside of place and time?" I whispered to her. "Yes, when I was on Loza's back. What about you? When you go swimming?"

"Maybe, sometimes, when I swim. Especially in the sea. But recently, since the Elephant left me . . ." Her voice broke. I didn't tell her about our conversation, and I just went on suppressing my anger at her impetuous, foolish ways.

"So," she went on, "I found out from a colleague that his wife took the children to her family for the school holidays. For hours I was thinking about him being alone at home—in his home—happy to be liberated from his family. And from me. I felt like a huge wave was coming at me and was about to bury me. It was 2:00 a.m. or maybe a bit after that, and I went out in my car, in my pajamas, and there I was in front of his closed door, in bare feet and crazy with sadness, somewhere outside of consciousness of who I was or where in the world I was. I have no idea if I was screaming or crying or silent, I just threw myself at the door like a beggar, drowning in the waves of the black ocean that I couldn't see. I would have still been there at sunrise if my sister hadn't come and dragged me away."

I gave her a stare. "Ghazaala! You don't have any sisters."

She smiled weakly. "I do have a sister; she is a sister because we were nursed by the same mother. I've never told you about her because the way she disappeared—so suddenly—was horribly painful for me. But she came to me as I was crouching completely devastated in front of the Elephant's door, and she looked exactly the way she did the last time I saw her. Such an imposing, commanding figure, even though she was only fourteen then. She was wearing our school uniform, and I think that was what she was wearing when she left Sharaat Bat without saying goodbye to me. In the darkness I could see her finger wagging at me, and then she lifted me up, from my underarms, just like the Violin Player did when he kissed me for the first time. She put me on her back—her shoulders are so wide—and I was breathing in that smell that was her special smell. I had the feeling that the pocket of her school pinafore was full of rocks, the way it always used to be, and I knew she would protect me. She put me down in the driver's seat and she got the motor of my car running. She closed the door and went away. And I came home."

The two of them had met after work in a café not too far from the office. He was wearing his usual gray trousers and a white shirt with muted blue stripes. He was seated on a green sofa. She was in her work clothes, black skirt and neutral blouse. She sat down across from him on a brown-beige chair.

"Don't think too much," he said. "Leave things to their natural course. Don't try to analyze or explain anything . . ."

Ghazaala studied the large poster on the wall behind him. A black-and-white image of an old street paved in stone with two old people crossing it.

He ordered a cappuccino; she did the same. He took a sip and tried to lick the foam off his lips. "Now we're friends," he said. "Nothing has happened."

Was this a real image hung behind him, a life-size image? Maybe . . .

"Do you see?" he asked. "We belong to two different worlds, we have different situations to deal with . . ."

She didn't like her coffee cold. She usually drank it quickly while it was still hot. He would laugh. "All in one swallow? It's coffee, not milk."

She couldn't pick up his scent, even though she was sitting directly across from him. If she were to stick out her foot, the tip of her shoe would touch his knee. He tipped his head back. "You know? I wasn't intending to put an end to our meetings. You are fantastic, but it's a dead end for us. Damn circumstances."

What song was it, blaring through the café speakers? She knew the latest trends in pop music but this didn't sound like it belonged. At home, she recalled, the twins sang a song something like this one, and they always tried to make her dance with them. Who would ever guess that they were twins? They didn't look at all alike, and they didn't even look like her. They delighted in going out with their father, as if he hadn't abandoned them for all those years. They would come home carrying bags of fast food, cans of soda, and things he had bought them that made a lot of noise. The wonderful, fabulous father was the one who didn't set any rules for two boys he saw at most once every two or three weeks. Meanwhile, it was the stern mother who filled their lives with rules.

"Yes, it's true," he went on. "You are such a splendid friend, and so impressive—how could anyone ever treat you poorly?

But it's circumstances, it's just life—you know. My daughter, Amina, goes through such awful spells of pain, hospital visits, problems with her hearing and her thyroid. The media do us wrong when they report that Down's syndrome children are all happy beings—what happiness is there in this misery that my wife and I live? You showed up at the wrong time . . ."

Or was that actually a photograph, a black-and-white photograph and not an artist's sketch after all? How old were those two stooped people? What did they have to say to each other? Little smiles played around both of their lips as if they were happy with whatever they had just said and happy about what they would say next.

"Don't give it too much thought, Layla. You know? Life is like that. And my wife, you know, she's very sensitive."

But she wasn't Layla. That person, Layla, existed only in official documents. Why had they put green banquettes in here along with the brown ones? Maybe a certain amount of green could go well with brown, but this much? She wasn't so sure.

"Why are you so difficult, Mama?" That's what the two of them said to her. "Papa never gives us lectures on how harmful the oils and sugar content at McDonald's are. He doesn't make us limit our PlayStation and iPad time. Papa's *cool*. We like going out with him." She only asked them one question about their father. It was all she wanted to know. "Does he still play music?" They said he sometimes played the violin in the evening. Was it the same instrument, she wondered. The one whose pinewood body he had loved, playing it in their little apartment. But she would never know.

"You know what? When I found out that I would be blessed with a daughter, after the boy, I was so happy. I didn't know what life was hiding away for us. Damn—damn this bint kalb life. Don't be angry, Layla. We'll still be friends. I wish you would say something."

She picked up her handbag and got to her feet. He put out his hand but she ignored it. Leaving the café, she saw the bird. It practically followed her. She knew what kind of bird it was. One of the migratory birds who passed by here for a short season. When one of these birds came to rest in the winter mountain region of her childhood, Saada would dab its head with olive oil and let it go on its way. Certain it would pass by the Tomb of the Prophet on its journey, she would ask it to convey greetings and love.

She drove to the sea. In the afternoon the beach was deserted. She took out the full-body swimsuit that never left the trunk of her car. She took off her skirt and blouse and tossed them on the sand. She threw herself into the waves. Maybe every human being had a certain share of love coming to them, and trying to demand any more than that was simply going too far. Maybe Ghazaala had been given her lot of love in childhood, and all of her miserable love affairs were nothing more than an attempt to regain the purity and depth of that early love. The love of Asiya and her mother, Saada.

She moved farther away from the shore. She didn't feel the sun above her. She dove into the sea's depths, swimming swimming swimming. She didn't allow her arms and legs to grow tired. If she gave in now, if she collapsed, Asiya would not come to save her. Asiya would not pull her out as she used to when Ghazaala got stuck in one of the narrow canals. She wouldn't grab on to her as she had done when Ghazaala dove into the muddy rainwater ponds. She pushed with her arms, and her afterbirth detached itself and floated away. Her screams returned—a nursing baby, abandoned until her mouth found Saada's chest. She kicked her legs, and all of the familiar rooms furnished with fragile care broke to pieces, dissolving into the waves along with the fragrances of Asiya and the bread baking at dawn and the twins' nappies. The shadows of faces, the echoes of laughter, the melodies of the violin—all of it scattered and disappeared inside the drops of water.

She needed to become one with the water. To become the water herself. The water knew her and was tender toward her. It bore the burden of the heart, the unbearable weight she carried. Now the waves were carrying it instead, and the burden floated and became transparent. Her arms pushed against the water—arms she had given to the Violin Player, had imagined for the Singer to the Queen, had amputated for the Elephant. But now here they were; they were for the water and nothing else. She floated on her back, letting the waves carry her. The waves understood that in her spirit there were rocks and pebbles and bits of iron weighing her down, but the waves did not let her sink. Did not let her drown. They lifted her and they deposited her gently onshore.

She stands facing the sea and she screams. She feels no thirst, no hunger, no fatigue. She screams for all that is suppressed and imprisoned, and she weeps. She screams for all of the tears that have been turned into stone by the pressures of behaving as one ought. She screams because she is herself, her own person; she screams and expels herself from her own lungs. She screams for mercy, she screams her pain. She screams out what she cannot reveal and screams out what she has revealed, screams for having revealed more than she should have. She screams her excuses and her apologies. She screams for all of the waiting, the expectations. She rips it all apart. She carves into it with a saw-edged knife so that it will hurt. She is the murderer and the knife. And you—you are what awaits, but you do not deserve to wait any longer for your death.

The sun goes down and Ghazaala slips back into the sea. Gazelle who is Layla but without a Qays to love her hopelessly and memorialize her in his ancient poetry. Layla who is Gazelle but without the long legs that would allow her to flee. Who is a fish but without the ability to adjust to life underwater, under the watercourse of life. She puts all her energy into her arms and legs, and she swims. She floats on the waves so she can stare into the black sky. She sees the stars that might themselves be long dead, but their light still arrives, calling out to Ghazaala's spirit.

JOKHA ALHARTHI was the first Omani woman to have a novel translated into English. *Celestial Bodies* went on to win the International Booker Prize and became an international bestseller. Alharthi is the author of three collections of short fiction, three children's books, and four novels in Arabic. She completed a PhD in classical Arabic poetry in Edinburgh and teaches at Sultan Qaboos University in Muscat.

MARILYN BOOTH is Emerita Khalid bin Abdullah Al Saud Chair for the Study of the Contemporary Arab World at Oxford University. In addition to her academic publications, she has translated many works of fiction from the Arabic. Recent titles include *No Road to Paradise* by Hassan Daoud, *Bitter Orange Tree* by Jokha Alharthi, *Voices of the Lost* by Hoda Barakat, and one of the first Arabic novels to be penned by a female author, Alice Butrus al-Bustani's *Sa'iba*, forthcoming in Oxford World's Classics. Her translation of Alharthi's *Celestial Bodies* won the 2019 International Booker Prize.